THE
MYTHOLOGY
of
MIDDLE-EARTH

THE
MYTHOLOGY
of
MIDDLE-EARTH

RUTH S. NOEL

HOUGHTON MIFFLIN COMPANY BOSTON

1978

Library of Congress Cataloging in Publication Data

Noel, Ruth S
  The mythology of Middle-earth.

  Bibliography: p.
  Includes index.
    1. Tolkien, John Ronald Reuel, 1892–1973—
Knowledge—Folk-lore, mythology. 2. Mythology in
literature. I. Title.
PR6039.032Z72   828'.9'1209   76–48162
ISBN 0–395–25006–4   ISBN 0–395–27208–4 pbk.

Printed in the United States of America

V 10 9 8 7 6 5 4 3 2 1

To my brother,

Jefferson Putnam Swycaffer

ACKNOWLEDGMENTS

THIS BOOK has been simmering — Tolkien, Frazer, Irish myths, etc. — for ten years. The catalyst was sent by my husband from a business trip, a book I had wanted but never asked for — the *New Larousse Encyclopedia of Mythology*.

Dr. Alfred Boc at San Diego State University read my first draft while it was still typed on file cards. He urged radical reorganization, emphasized Aragorn's similarity to King Arthur, and explained the dream phenomenon behind subterranean descent. Uncharacteristically, I took all his advice.

Greg Bear, science fiction author and illustrator, encouraged me and lent me books. Patty Knox, a graduate linguist, read the next-to-final manuscript and made valuable suggestions. Jeff Swycaffer, my brother, proofread numerous drafts, discussed tirelessly, and pointed out the similarities between Aragorn and Charlemagne.

My husband, Greg Noel, edited countless drafts with considerable patience and insight, contributing greatly to the organization of the book. I took pity on him and wrote the final draft alone, so neither he nor any of the other contributors are responsible for any defects or errors, but all deserve heartfelt thanks.

*

CONTENTS

PART V . THINGS (CONT.)

PART
I

INTRODUCTION

INTRODUCTION

THERE IS SOMETHING in Professor John Ronald Reuel Tolkien's works that lies deeper than fantasy or escape. This quality is the same as that found in authentic myths and folk tales, a sense generated by the nearly forgotten but potent beliefs and traditions that form the skeleton of old lore. Researchers such as Sir James Frazer have compared and explicated some of these sources, tracing great epics and bedtime stories alike back to the first human struggles to bring order to the world. The sense of depth in Tolkien's works has its source in the author's understanding and selective use of the ancient themes from mythology.

This book relates Tolkien's works to the mythic themes upon which they are based. The introduction discusses some of the purposes of myth, the effect of myth on the development of Middle-earth, and Tolkien's philosophies on myth.

Although primarily a philologist, Tolkien studied mythology for most of his life. He was one of the world's greatest authorities on the Old English and Middle English languages, and was a specialist in Old English and related Teutonic and Celtic lore. With his works he made an eminently successful effort to revive the decreasing interest in mythology. The Teutonic and Celtic mythologies that most interested Tolkien

4   INTRODUCTION

had never been given the emphasis that had been placed upon classical Greek and Roman mythology; Tolkien's works have helped to arouse interest in these areas. This can be seen in the number of recent works based on these myths.

To thoroughly appreciate Tolkien's works, it is necessary to have an understanding of mythology. Unfortunately, the study of mythology itself is a very uncertain one, and it is seldom possible to reconstruct a single clear-cut version of a myth with its sources and purposes neatly set out. Contemporary records of pre-Christian myths are often contradictory or confused. Later accounts of these myths are more coherent, but both the conversion to Christianity and the effort of organizing the material have often biased the telling of ancient lore. So much has been lost from Celtic and Teutonic mythology that it is doubtful that a single, fundamental, and coherent interpretation will ever be made of what remains. Trends in interpretation change, new material is discovered, and, on occasion, old material is found to be unreliable. Only rarely does a comprehensive, scientific inquiry, such as that of Jakob and Wilhelm Grimm into Teutonic mythology, or a dedicated, gifted retelling of the myths, like that of the twelfth-century Icelandic writer Snorri Sturluson, bring mythology alive to the reader.

The understanding of mythology requires the understanding of its purposes. The purposes of mythology are to glorify history with supernatural events, to explain the unknown, and to hallow tradition. First, historical myths augment history with supernatural events and divine beings, suggesting that the civilization concerned has been singled out for divine guidance. Second, myths that explain the unknown attempt to bring order to a chaotic conception of the world and to provide formal answers to questions that cannot be answered practically. Third, myths that hallow tradition describe the supernatural circumstances in which the traditions came about, glorifying the traditions in order to perpetuate them. Comparable mythologies have evolved in virtually every culture because man universally faces the same challenges, asks the same questions, and lives in awe of the same forces.

There are two levels of myth in *The Lord of the Rings*. Not only is it written as an epic myth itself, but it also presents the internal mythologies of the peoples of Middle-earth. The three basic purposes of myth are served in these internal mythologies. The histories are peopled with divine and immortal beings, questions about the unknown are given answers, and traditions are hallowed and maintained.

Tolkien was aware of mythology's purposes and used it meaningfully. His fidelity to the purposes of myth produces a coherent internal mythology for the epic of Middle-earth and provides significant depth for the characterization of both individuals and nations.

Tolkien's adaptation of mythology to his works has a profound effect on the reader. This effectiveness is not accidental. Mythic themes deal with basic challenges that face man universally and eternally, such as love, fate, and death. Mythic thought is traceable to the very emergence of human imagination. Such symbolism can be seen in Paleolithic art with its records of ceremonial events and its expressionistic depiction of nature. Even earlier symbolism can be seen in Neanderthal burials, in which the manner of burial was determined by some dawning concept of an afterlife, or imaginative attempt at restoration of life to the dead.

Mythological themes are vastly ancient and are a basic part of the subconscious working of the mind. Thus they have the power to thrill or terrify in the same way that

dreams do. In fact, the symbols common in mythology sometimes arise spontaneously in dreams. The study of psychology
is doing much to explain the motivation of mythic themes.

Because of the powerful connotation of myth, Tolkien
considered mythic themes the most effective way to glorify
or debase his characters. An independent author, seldom influenced by his contemporaries, Tolkien must have used his
own reactions as a basis for choosing his mythological themes.
Sometimes his selections are questionable, such as the apparent
death of nearly every important character. Other themes,
however, produce a stifling, nightmare horror or a spiritual
sense of exultation. The considerable popularity of Tolkien's
works attests to the appeal of his selections.

Although the sources of many of Tolkien's themes are to
be found in mythology, specific influences are sometimes
difficult to trace. Sometimes the theme's source, such as that
of the fragment about the otter (discussed in the section on
Bombadil) can be located with certainty. Sometimes the
theme, such as that of Sauron's powerful, lost Ring, is ubiquitous so that it is difficult to determine a particular source.
Sometimes the ideas, such as those concerning the nature of
the Elves and Dwarves, are so general that they do not seem
to have come from a single source, but rather to have been
absorbed through a sort of literary osmosis. In cases of the
latter kind, this book will discuss the various occurrences of
the theme. It is not intended that all the references should be
taken as direct influences on Tolkien's writing. On the other
hand, it is more than likely that Tolkien was familiar with all
of them.

Tolkien's works form a continuation of the mythic tradition into modern literature. For this reason they form a genre
by themselves. In no other literary work has such a careful

balance of mythic tradition and individual imagination been maintained. Authors who have been compared with Tolkien emphasize either the mythic or the imaginative side of their works to the detriment of the other. Tolkien, however, maintains a consistent homogeneity.

Throughout the works, the fiction is maintained that the prehistoric chronology of the Third Age of Middle-earth is the source of the mythologies we know. Tolkien excuses his use of names and themes from historic mythology on the basis that *The Lord of the Rings* tells the true story, imperfectly remembered in our historic lore. Bilbo's song, "There is an inn," sung by Frodo, is a good example: Tolkien presents what he pretends is the original form of the nursery rhyme, "Hey diddle diddle," where the cow jumps over the moon.

The adaptation of mythological themes to imaginative fiction is a difficult challenge. Mythology is a conservative medium: myths are always repeated in a traditional way, rather than being casually left to the teller's whim. However, the constant retelling of myths over hundreds, even thousands, of years wears them smooth, concentrates them, until everything superfluous is worn away. In contrast, modern literature is dependent on innovation and creativity for its success. In combining the two literary philosophies, Tolkien produced a myth that is coherent and readable from the modern point of view, and a work of imaginative fiction made concrete by its basis in the ancient and universal language of myth. The result of the combination is sometimes self-conscious, forced, and unwieldy, but much of it is remarkably vivid, dimensional, and evocative.

The success of Tolkien's works is based on the vividness, dimensionality, and evocative qualities of Middle-earth. To say Middle-earth was created by Tolkien would be an oversimplification. Instead, Middle-earth exists on three levels. First, it is the actual continent of Europe, with landscapes, vegetation, animal life, and some of man's ancient works, taken from reality. Second, Middle-earth is the product of the poetic imagination of the early Europeans, who peopled the mountains, forest, and sea with divine, semidivine, and demonic beings. Finally, Tolkien superimposed his imagination on the lands and their natural and supernatural inhabitants, enhancing the mood of the landscape and deepening the character of its peoples.

Whatever Middle-earth is, it is not Faerie. It is not, as Faerie is said to be, a remote, inviolable land of indescribable beauty. There are isolated fragments of Faerie, or rather reconstructions of it, in Tolkien's Middle-earth, in such places as Lórien. On the whole, however, there is very little of the supernatural in the geography of Middle-earth.

Nevertheless, there is a curiously timeless quality about Middle-earth. Its history spans thousands of years, and the time of the War of the Ring is apparently both prehistoric and pagan, although the primary culture is feudal and such anachronisms as coffee and potatoes have intruded. This sense of mingled time-frames is reminiscent of that of Malory's *Le Morte Darthur*, a resemblance that may not be accidental. In *Le Morte Darthur*, myths about Celtic gods are attributed to the approximately fifth-century King Arthur, but are set in the culture and language of medieval chivalry. The result in both Malory's and Tolkien's works is a curiously opposite suspension of time. *The Lord of the Rings* appears to have the timelessness the hobbits ascribed to Lórien: "as if inside a song" — a medieval song sung to a pagan tune.

The best available guide to what Tolkien felt about the mythology that inspired his works is found in his essay "On

Fairy-Stories." Tolkien wrote this essay at the time he was beginning *The Lord of the Rings*, and it later appeared in the book *Tree and Leaf*. In view of the way *The Lord of the Rings* finally developed, the essay's insights on magic, *eucatastrophe*, and justice are particularly valuable.

The magic Tolkien admired was magic devoid of sleight-of-hand fakery, mystery uncontaminated by cloak-and-dagger sensationalism, and miracle unconfined to orthodox religion. The purpose of this magic is to exercise the sense of wonder and to fulfill wish. Magic is the process which produces eucatastrophe.

Eucatastrophe is Tolkien's word for the anti-catastrophic "turn" (*strophe* in Greek) that characterizes fairy stories. This turning occurs when imminent evil is unexpectedly averted and great good succeeds. To Tolkien, tragedy was the purest form of drama, while eucatastrophe, the antithesis of tragedy, was the purest form of the fairy story. In "On Fairy-Stories," Tolkien gives the purpose and effect of eucatastrophe: "It does not deny the existence . . . of sorrow and failure . . . it denies universal final defeat . . . giving a fleeting glimpse of Joy, Joy beyond the walls of the world, poignant as grief."

To Tolkien, the most satisfying form of eucatastrophe, and that which he developed to the greatest extent in his works, was denial of death. This concept is basic to Christianity, but also plays an important part in pagan myth. The desire for eternal life runs deep in the human imagination — burial practices of even some Neanderthal peoples reflect a hope of life beyond the grave. Sometimes, as in Scandinavian mythology, the afterlife was visualized as a continuation of earthly life: in Odin's hall, warriors fought and feasted until the end of the world. The fighting and feasting were an important part of the Celtic afterlife as well, but the Celts added a significant element in their lyrical descriptions of the unearthly beauty and joy of the otherworld. However, it is not the physical aspect of the afterworld, or the events that take place there, that are important. (Tolkien wisely gave only the most sparse account of the Blessed Realm.) The need is to believe, even briefly or metaphorically, that death can be denied, even with the recognition of the necessary departure from the living world. This is the eucatastrophe from old lore which Tolkien has striven to supply.

Another theme that Tolkien found in fairy stories was justice. In his own works, it is unfailingly meted out, although he sparingly doles out the deepest doom, death, never giving it to any character introduced by name except as punishment for inexpiable sins or as a victorious resolution of all life's conflicts.

Tolkien's adherence to justice and mercy is his greatest concession to the Christian philosophy. For a dedicatedly Christian author, Tolkien wrote an unusually sympathetic account of a pagan world. The combination is again reminiscent of Malory's *Le Morte Darthur*, where pagan themes, motives, and moods are interspersed with Christian ideals.

Despite Tolkien's statement to the contrary, justice is not inherent in fairy stories. For example, he said that "The Frog Prince" is about the importance of keeping promises. In the version collected by Jakob and Wilhelm Grimm, the princess indeed promised the frog a place by her dish and on her pillow if he recovered her golden ball. But when he came for his reward, she angrily dashed him against the wall. He became a prince thereupon, and married the disloyal and undeserving princess. This sort of caprice of fate is as common in folk tales as is justice.

The emphasis on fate rather than on justice is as much the hallmark of modernism in literature as it was of pre-Christian myth. It is no longer necessary for a work of fiction to come to a conclusion that satisfies the desire for justice or mercy. It is not even necessary to reach any resolution. The same effect occurs in myth when the favor of the gods is bestowed or withdrawn arbitrarily. This point of view is one of realism: justice and mercy are less facts than spiritual ideals.

Tolkien demonstrated this in his overall view of the quest, where he showed justice to be a goal — unrealized but attainable. He gave two roles to justice in view of his combination of pagan fatalism and Judeo-Christian ethics. In the pagan sense, justice is to be striven for so that one may meet fate honorably. In the Judeo-Christian sense, it is sought in order that one may reject evil. Appropriately to these two roles, Tolkien resolved the story in two directions, with the idealist, Frodo, departing to eternal life beyond the world, and the realist, Samwise, returning to the center of the world's life, the hearth of home.

PART
II

THEMES

THEMES

THERE ARE several themes that extend throughout Tolkien's works, the warp threads of their structure. They are basic to myth and give scope and detail to Tolkien's writing. These major themes are fate, subterranean descent, denial of death, language, and chronology. These themes, outlined here, will be analyzed in depth in succeeding chapters.

The concept of predestined fate is found frequently in myth. In Tolkien's works the question of predestination and free will is unresolved. There are pivotal events when the characters choose between possible courses, but even then they are guided by the Guardians of the World.

Subterranean descent is the significant turning of the story line out of the sunlight world. The action descends into an unlit realm of terror and triumph. This theme has a dreamlike effect, both for the reader and for the characters.

Denied death is the highest form of eucatastrophe, the sudden, unexpected turning of a story from sorrow into joy. The most satisfying form of this turning occurs when anticipated death is averted, providing hope for the eternal, universal denial of death.

Language is important to the detailed view of Middle-earth. As a philologist, Tolkien used language as a way of depicting the natures of the many peoples of Middle-earth — their relationships and differences.

Chronology, time, and calendars are given a curious emphasis in Tolkien's works. A great deal of mythology is associated with calendric systems and the measurement of time in general. Tolkien used chronology as one of his most unusual devices for overlaying *The Lord of the Rings* with realistic detail.

I

Fate

LITERATURE based on a belief in predestined fate provides a sense of inevitability and of man's subordination to forces beyond his control. Both myth and Tolkien's works are based on this concept of destiny. However, free will plays some part in Tolkien's works, and circumstances arise when fate is dependent upon choice.

Throughout pre-Christian mythology, fate is an overwhelming force. Many of the Scandinavian myths form a pattern — in them certain foredoomed events, predicted but inescapable, herald the inevitable twilight of the gods. Teutonic mythology is permeated by the concept that fate is stronger even than the gods and will overcome them.

A similar sense of tragic destiny is often seen in the Irish tales where there was a system of *geissi*, supernatural prohibitions which, when broken, led to evil fortune or death. The Irish heroes were always eventually placed in a position in which they must break the *geissi*, either unintentionally or for their survival. The very existence of such a system demonstrates belief in predestined fate.

One significant way of depicting fate in myth was through personifications. Throughout European mythology there are widespread myths of Fates, Norns, and Fays. These supernatural wisewomen determined the destiny of individuals, spinning or weaving the threads of life, lighting life's candles, or decreeing the fate of the newborn.

Fate was often seen through the eyes of an omniscient being. For example, in the "Völuspâ," the first poem of the *Elder Edda*, the seeress Vala described the details of the origin, the inevitable destruction, and the rebirth of the world, indicating the degree to which the fate of the world was predetermined.

In *The Lord of the Rings* the Guardians of the World, the Valar, invoked certain rules and prohibitions on the peoples of Middle-earth. It was their decree, for example, that the Ring must stay in Middle-earth and not be brought into the West. In many cases the Valar determined the pattern of events. This is what Gandalf meant when he said that Bilbo had been meant to find the Ring and that Gollum would still play a fateful part in the Ring's history. The intervention of the Valar is also suggested at such times as when Frodo accepted the quest of the Ring, feeling that another will spoke with his voice.

One medium through which fate is learned in myth is that of prophecy. Throughout the Arthurian Cycle, for example, future events are often anticipated in detail. Merlin, and the mysterious old men who took his place after his imprisonment, consistently prophesied events that involved a variety of persons, weapons, and landmarks. Moreover, prophecies were often found written, by no human agency, on swords and tombs.

Tolkien's works also contain many prophecies. Gandalf frequently knew or felt "in his heart" the consequences of an event or the future of a person or creature. Added to this, he had consistent visions of far-off events. The Elves and the Dúnedain also made important prophecies. Another significant prophetic medium in *The Lord of the Rings*, the *palantíri*, or the Seeing-stones, showed visions not only of the past and the distant present, but of the future as well.

Several prophecies appeared in the folklore of Middle-earth. In *The Hobbit* it was recorded that the men of Lake-town maintained a tradition that the Dwarf-king would eventually re-establish his realm beneath the Mountain. In *The Lord of the Rings* the old wives in Gondor repeated a rhyme about the curative powers of the herb *athelas:* ". . . Life for the dying/In the king's hand lying." They also believed that the king, when he returned, would be recognized for his healing hands.

Prophetic dreams occur frequently in myth. The stories of Joseph and Pharaoh and of Daniel and Nebuchadnezzar are famous examples. Such dreams occur in *The Lord of the Rings* as well. Frodo, sleeping in the house of Bombadil, not only dreamed about Gandalf being rescued from Orthanc, days after the event, but also dreamed about the voyage he himself was fated to make to the Blessed Realm. The dream that came to Faramir and Boromir was more specific: "Seek for the Sword that was broken . . ." — it directed Boromir so that he arrived in Rivendell on the morning the fateful council of Elrond was to convene.

The fate of Middle-earth was not entirely predestined. The outcome of certain events could be determined by the choice of individuals. For example, Frodo, on Amon Hen, caught between opposing wills, had a moment in which he was free to make his own choice.

The Mirror of Galadriel also suggested a capricious combination of fate and will. It not only showed a predetermined future, but also suggested futures that were to take place only under certain conditions.

A curious prophecy combining destiny and free will was made by Malbeth the Seer, who gave Arvedui ("Last King") his name at birth. He foretold that Arvedui would have one of two possible fates, to be determined by the choices of the Dúnedain. He said Arvedui was destined either to become the last king of the North Kingdom, or to change his name and rule both Arnor and Gondor.

The variety of ways in which fatedness is indicated in Middle-earth, and the fact that, for the most part, superior beings are responsible for this fate, endows Tolkien's works with some of the pagan mood of the Celtic and Scandinavian myths. The inevitabilities of the world are glimpsed, and the courage of Tolkien's heroes, like that of the ancient heroes, exists in their determination to devote all their energy to meeting that fate honorably.

2

Subterranean Descent

SUBTERRANEAN DESCENT forms a recurring theme in Tolkien's works. It removes the action of the story from the natural world into "the deep places of the world" where extraordinary events occur. In almost every instance of this theme in Tolkien's works, the descent is accompanied by a deep sensation of dread, by an encounter with a terrifying supernatural creature, and by an unexpected, valuable achievement.

These descents have the quality and function of dreams. The descent itself corresponds to the transition from waking to dreaming. The feeling of apprehension or terror is that of nightmare, intense and unreasoning. The supernatural creatures resemble the hardly recognizable symbols that appear in dreams, signifying the challenges in waking life. The achievements come with the defeat of the beast, as the comprehension of a dream's symbols can serve as a guide to the unexpected attainment of a goal.

The Hobbit contains several variations of the descent theme. In them, the dread is not as intense as in those in *The Lord of the Rings*, and the things achieved in the descent tend to be more material.

The travelers' first dangerous encounter was with the Trolls. When the Trolls were vanquished, the adventurers entered the Trolls' cave. They felt very uneasy there, but brought out the Trolls' treasure hoard. In it were swords essential to the development of the story.

The next descent, into the goblin-holes in the Misty Mountains, actually began with a dream — Bilbo's dream that a crack had opened in the back of the cave where the travelers sheltered. The descent was dark, confused, and frightening, and Bilbo was threatened both by goblins and Gollum. However, through no effort of his own he came upon the Ring, then won the riddle game with Gollum, and escaped.

The events in the tunnel-like paths of Mirkwood were also dreamlike, dark, and interminable. One piece of bad luck followed the other in a surreal sequence. Monsters were represented by giant spiders; in conquering them, Bilbo won the sincere respect of the Dwarves for the first time.

When the company was imprisoned in Thranduil's subterranean halls, their only adversary was the unjustly suspicious Elven-king. The Elves' fortress underground, guarded by magic doors, is paralleled in myths and folk tales. Mythic Elves as well as Dwarves were credited with living underground. They, as well as ogres and sorcerers, often had their dwellings protected by similar magic.

The adventurers' escape was mythic as well. Effected by casks on a river, it resembles symbolic journeys of rebirth. Such journeys afloat on leaves, in baskets, or in chests are common in folk tales and are also found in such myths as those of Perseus and Moses. In the case of the Dwarves, the rebirth consisted of escaping a place where they were considered criminals to one where they were hailed as heroes led by a king destined to fulfill a prophecy.

The most typical descents were those in which Bilbo entered the deep halls under the Lonely Mountain and confronted the dragon alone. He did so twice, the first time returning with a precious cup, the second time discovering the dragon's weak point, thus indirectly helping to win back the ancestral kingdom and treasure for the Dwarves, as well as notable wealth for himself.

In *The Lord of the Rings*, the descents take on a heightened quality of terror and the achievements are less material than those in *The Hobbit*. More attention is given to the emotional elements and to the effect on the characters. The entire quest is not one to find treasure, as in *The Hobbit*, but to destroy one in order to win a more precious freedom. As a result, the ethical aspects of the quest are emphasized.

In the first subterranean sequence in *The Fellowship of the Ring*, the hobbits confronted a supernatural wight in a barrow and nearly succumbed to its paralyzing spell. Here Frodo first demonstrated his true courage, overcoming the temptation to use the Ring for his own escape. Instead he attacked the murderous dead hand that threatened his companions, and called Tom Bombadil. When summoned, Bombadil let the sunlight into the barrow and broke the sleeping-spell on the other hobbits. He arrived with dreamlike swiftness, but woke the travelers to reality.

The sequence in Moria is probably the most dramatic of the descents, although it is told in two parts. The first part describes the long lightless journey, the duel with the vast and terrifying Balrog, and Gandalf's fall. It is not until the next volume that the achievement is disclosed: the Balrog's destruction and Gandalf's rebirth in a more powerful aspect, able to vanquish Saruman and the emissaries of the Dark Lord.

A less characteristic descent is Gimli's discovery of the Glittering Caves during the battle at Helm's Deep. This descent is not into a fearful place inhabited by monsters, but into a place of beauty and refuge. The event is significant, however, in that Gimli founded a Dwarf-realm there after the War of the Rings. The battle takes the place of a dream monster and Gimli's realm is the thing achieved.

Like the account of Moria, Aragorn's descent into the Paths of the Dead is told in two parts. The first part describes the warning against the Paths, the terror of the darkness and the Dead, the oath at the Stone of Erech, and the lightless ride of the living and the Dead across Gondor. The second half describes the achievement: the defeat of the Corsairs and the triumphal ride of the Dúnedain up the Anduin River to release Minas Tirith from siege.

Samwise, after penetrating the tunnels of Shelob's Lair, achieved a turning point in his life when he vanquished the giant spider-thing. This major demonstration of courage increased his capability. From that point on he assumed a leading role, rescuing Frodo from the Orcs and guiding him through Mordor as Frodo became overpowered by the influence of the Ring.

The final challenge and climax of *The Lord of the Rings* took place in the Chambers of Fire in Mount Doom. There Frodo faced both the baleful influence of the Enemy and the cataclysmic completion of his task. The quest was ultimately achieved, but through an unanticipated series of events.

Descents of this type have an important role in myth, where they often provide important turning points. Sometimes they consist of a journey by a living hero into the underworld to obtain counsel or rescue the dead. (The counsel is usually oracular and the attempt at rescuing the dead is usually unsuccessful.) The descent sequences in myth are almost always pervaded by an unreal, dreamlike quality. One of the most curious, with which Tolkien was well-acquainted, is the descent by Beowulf into the lake of monsters to kill Grendel's mother. Beowulf descended through the water for hours before reaching the bottom and engaging the monster in battle. This journey is far more unreal than those into a merely subterranean underworld. The whole sequence is impossible, even to the gushing of hot blood from the body of the long-dead Grendel. However, immediately after Beowulf returned to shore, he re-entered the world of reality. His companions were suddenly concerned with practical problems, such as the transportation of Beowulf's armor and of Grendel's huge head. The same sense of unreality is present in Tolkien's descent sequences, as is the subsequent return to practical reality after the achievement of an important goal.

3

Denial of Death

IF DEATH is what mortals fear most, then the denial of the finality of death must be their greatest desire. Awe of death and the attempt to return some semblance of life to the corpse form the first known examples of the conception of the supernatural in prehistoric peoples. When mythology developed, the hope of eluding death took such forms as accounts of supernatural immortals whose lives need never end, of semidivine ancestral peoples with incredible life-spans, and of the anticipation of some life after death.

Tolkien's works include all these forms. The Valar were both divine and undying, while the Elves, their chief worshipers, were immortal. The Númenoreans, ancestors of the Dúnedain of Arnor and Gondor, were very long-lived, but as they came to covet immortality their life-spans dwindled. Nevertheless, the Dúnedain of the North at the time of the War of the Ring were still much longer lived than other men. The Dwarves of Middle-earth reached comparably great ages, probably on account of the mythic depiction of Dwarves as greybeards. Part of the appeal of the hobbits is their long lives; these never equaled those of the Dúnedain or the Dwarves, but hobbits often reached one hundred years of age. Beyond the world, across the Western Seas, the Blessed Realm offered an eternal life for the Elves and the few mortals chosen by the Valar. Besides this, the tales of Arwen and Elessar and of Lúthien and Beren hinted at some other form of life after death beyond the confines of the earth.

Tolkien emphasized the escape from death, and made apparent death and subsequent recovery a recurring theme in his works. Approximately twenty such apparent deaths occur; in fact, Frodo was thought dead six times. Bilbo, Bard, Pippin, Merry, Samwise, Aragorn, Faramir, Éowyn and Bill the pony were all also thought dead one or more times, but were unexpectedly found alive or were healed when near death. Gandalf indeed died after destroying the Balrog. But he was sent back into the world, apparently by the Valar, to complete his quest.

The most satisfying eucatastrophe occurs when death is eluded entirely and immortal life substituted. This highest form of escape from death was bestowed upon the Ringbearers and the Guardians of the Elven Rings when they sailed into the West to the Undying Lands. Although they went beyond death to the Blessed Realm, the travelers went beyond the living world as well, and endured a poignant separation from their lands and kin. Tolkien believed that such mingling of joy and grief is the characteristic resolution in the most memorable of the world's lore.

4

Language

AN EXPERT PHILOLOGIST, Tolkien had a virtuoso control of language. He changed the type of English he used to suit the characters or events of his works, he created consistent languages for a variety of peoples, and he engaged in complex word-play. The languages reinforce Tolkien's depiction of the peoples through the sounds they use, indicate the relationships between other speakers and the hobbits, and clarify the interrelationships of various peoples.

Tolkien consistently suggested the natures of the various peoples of Middle-earth through the sounds of their languages. (No less than fifteen different languages appear in Tolkien's works, excluding Modern and Middle English.) The musical flow of Elvish words and names implies that the Elves were a noble people with a love of beauty and music. The guttural, unfamiliar sound of Dwarvish indicates how completely that language was isolated from that of men and Elves. The prolonged woodwind chants of the Ents demonstrate their unhurried life as a part of the forest. The croaked curses of the Orcs establish them as a coarse, cruel, unimaginative folk.

Tolkien used English to represent the Common Speech, Westron, spoken by the hobbits and most of the Free Peoples of Middle-earth. The relationship of English to the languages of other peoples indicates those peoples' relationship to the hobbits. Throughout most of *The Lord of the Rings*, Anglo-Saxon-based English is used to give the effect of simple dignity and proximity to nature. In the Shire, the English Tolkien used was informal and often unsophisticated and provincial. In Rohan, actual Old English words, names, and phrases were used to show that their relationship to Modern English reflects the similarities between the tongues of the Shire and the Mark. These two languages had a common source in the speech of the men of Wilderland where both the hobbits and Rohirrim originated. In Gondor, French and other Latin-based words were used to suggest a language still more removed and noble than the Common Speech used elsewhere. This was because the inhabitants of Gondor spoke not only Westron but Elvish as well.

The relationships between peoples in *The Lord of the Rings* can also be seen in their vocabularies. The Quendi and Sindar, two branches of Elves with a common source, had many words in common as well as a larger vocabulary of related (cognate) words. The Elven tongues were also used by the faithful Númenoreans who founded Gondor; thus the Common Speech in Gondor retained much of the Elvish vocabulary. The proximity of the Men of Gondor even influenced the language of the Orcs of Mordor. For example, the Orcs used the word *Tark* to mean a man of Gondor. In origin, *tark* is an abbreviated form of the Quenya word *Tarcil* meaning "one of Númenorean descent."

Most of the names and titles of persons, places, and things, other than those in Modern, Middle, or Old English, are in Sindarin or Quenya Elvish. Sindarin (which means "Grey-elven") was the language of the Elves living west of the Anduin. In fact, most of the Elves, Rangers, and Stewards of

Gondor had Sindarin names, such as Aragorn, Denethor, and Galadriel. Quenya was the ceremonial language of both the Elves and the Dúnedain. The royal names of Gondor's kings were in Quenya, as the names of the faithful monarchs in Númenor had been. Elessar and Elendil are Quenya names.

A noticeable stylistic device of Tolkien's is the giving of a number of names and titles (often in different languages) to nearly every person, place, or thing. Aragorn, for example, is known by at least twelve different appellations. This system of multiple names is comparable to the poetic device called kennings, used in Teutonic poetry. Kennings form a complex pattern for providing alternate names. Sometimes these are descriptive. For example, the sea is called "whale road" and "swan road." Sometimes kennings alluded to mythology, gold being "the worm's bed" and "Fródi's meal" (these myths are discussed in later chapters).

Many of the allusions made by kennings are explained in the Icelandic *Prose Edda* and *Elder Edda*, to which there are many references in this book. The *Prose Edda* was written as a handbook for poets and explicated the allusions made in common kennings. A list of kennings for such natural objects as the moon and the sea appears in the *Elder Edda*. These kennings were used in a story told to Thór by a Dwarf and were supposed to represent the things as named in the languages of men, gods, giants, Elves, and Dwarves. The tradition that these different peoples had separate languages may have suggested Middle-earth's variety of tongues to Tolkien.

In developing these languages, Tolkien also provided alphabets in which to write them. His alphabets are a scholarly attempt at an aesthetic and consistent linguistic notation in which the forms of the letters indicate the relationship between their sounds. For example, the *Tengwar* are arranged so that the dentals have an open bow to the right, the labials have a closed bow to the right, voiced sounds have a double bow, etc. This organization is ingenious, but the symbols are too similar to one another for extended practical use.

As the *Tengwar* were ascribed by Tolkien to Fëanor in Eldamar in the Elder Days, so most ancient alphabets are associated with myths and ascribed to supernatural beings. The Teutonic runes, which form the basis for Tolkien's runes, are no exception. According to the *Elder Edda*, Teutonic runes were discovered and brought to mankind by the god Odin. Odin hung by the neck on the world-tree Yggdrasil for nine nights and days as a sacrifice to himself. At the end of this time he perceived runes lying below him. With a great effort he lifted them. Their power freed him from the tree and renewed his strength.

Rune means "secret" and the individual shape of runes was held to be an incantation. Certain single runes represented the names of gods and were used as appeals to them. When men invoked Tyr, the Teutonic sky-god, for help in battle, they engraved his initial ⇑ on their weapons. This appropriate runic character for T represents a barbed spear.

Tolkien used Old English runes in *The Hobbit* for their antiquity and atmosphere of magic and mystery, not to mention the fact that it is fairly easy to puzzle out an English message written in these runes. It was probably for the same reasons of atmosphere that he used the forms of runes for the *Cirth*, the Elf- and Dwarf-runes in *The Lord of the Rings*, although the organization of their forms, like that of the *Tengwar*, has phonetic significance.

A common element in Tolkien's works is word-play. This appears in the assimilation of words from ancient languages, in puns, and in riddles.

Tolkien often employed ancient words in his stories. Sometimes this had a calculated incongruous effect, as in his use of names from the *Eddas* for characters in *The Hobbit* and of would-be magnificent Latin titles among the country folk of *Farmer Giles of Ham*. Sometimes the similarity of sound between words in *The Lord of the Rings* and ancient words is used to suggest antiquity and remoteness. For example, the name of the beacon-hill Min-rimmon was probably suggested by Plinlimmon, the beacon-hill in the Welsh story of *Kilwch and Olwen*. The Strand of Ilmarin recalls the smith Ilmarinen in the Finnish *Kalevala*. The Stone of Erech may have been suggested by the existence of a Sumerian city of that name. Sir Dinadan and Sir Balin in the Arthurian Cycle may have inspired the title Dúnadan and the Dwarf-name Balin.

Tolkien used word-play in promoting the idea that *The Lord of the Rings* describes an age dimly remembered in historical vocabularies. This helps to arouse the reader's interest when words from historical contexts are used. For example, he used the Old English words *ent* and *orc* for highly specific types of creature, which he suggests were only vaguely or inaccurately remembered in Old English mythology. Tolkien often gave historical words a misleading meaning for the sake of a pun. For example, he made "the Cracks of Doom" (traditionally meaning the signal for the Day of Judgment) into a physical landmark — fissures in the interior of Mount Doom, where, as it happened, a type of day of judgment took place. Waybread, too, is a European plant whose name has nothing to do with bread, but makes a corrupted reference to its "broad" leaves. Quickbeam is a name for the rowan tree which refers not to speed, but to the rowan's reputed magic power to quicken new life.

Tolkien occasionally used words in the languages of Middle-earth which had a related meaning in an ancient tongue. The result is a sort of bilingual pun. As an example, *Vala* is the Quenya word for an angelic power and the Old Norse word for a seeress. Mordor is the Sindarin word for Black Country and the Old English word for murder or mortal sin. The name of Saruman's tower, Orthanc, had significant meanings both in the language of the Elves ("Mount Fang") and in Old English ("Cunning Mind"). In addition, all the Middle and Old English names of people and places in *The Lord of the Rings* have appropriate meanings. One example will suffice: the Mering Stream, forming part of the border between Rohan and Gondor. *Mering* is Old English for "forming a boundary."

A characteristic form of Tolkien's word-play is seen in the riddle game played by Bilbo and Gollum. It may seem incongruous that two such enemies should duel for their lives with a game of riddles, but there are precedents in ancient myth. Tales exist about Teutonic gods playing the riddle game with Giants and Dwarves for considerable wagers, even for lives. Once, when Odin, in disguise, riddled with the proud giant Vafthrudnir, he won by cheating intentionally, asking, not a riddle, but a question that only he as Odin could answer. In comparison, Bilbo never intended to cheat Gollum when he asked about the contents of his pocket. However, the solution of Bilbo's game may well have been suggested to Tolkien by Odin's artifice.

Also characteristic of Tolkien's virtuosity in language, Bilbo's riddle game is in rhyme. Tolkien realized the importance of poetic forms to myth, which was often traditionally told in a fixed meter. In fact the entire *Lord of the Rings* exhibits a poet's exhaustive care in choice of words, rhythm, and connotation. Tolkien used different rhyme schemes as he used different languages, ranging from chants for occasions of deep emotion, to intricate forms for ancient lore, to simple songs purely for enjoyment.

The uses of language form one of the most complex parts of the vast puzzle provided by Tolkien's works. Time after time he casually drops in a word or name of considerable mythic significance, and, just as often, pretends significance in words that are or were commonplace. Part of the puzzle arises from Tolkien's sharing a jest with his colleagues, part from his desire to arouse interest in linguistics, but most from his own sheer enjoyment of language.

5

Chronology

THE CHRONOLOGY in Tolkien's works is unusually coherent and consistent. It extends, in detail, over a period of more than six thousand years. Successive calendric systems of Middle-earth are described in depth. Dates and events are calculated with painstaking correlation to the regular cycles of the sun and moon. The consistency of the chronology adds considerably to the effect of realism in *The Lord of the Rings*, of the antiquity of Middle-earth's traditions, and of the impression of fatedness: events flow simultaneously to a single culmination, independently but inexorably.

The history of Middle-earth is placed long before recorded history. The dates have no relation to dates in historic systems and should not be used to postulate that *The Lord of the Rings* is a future history.

Four ages of the world are mentioned. The First Age (the Elder Days) ended with the overthrow of Morgoth. The Second Age was marked by the growing power of the Númenóreans in the West and of Sauron in the East. The age ended when the Last Alliance of Elves and men threw down Sauron, and Isildur claimed the Enemy's Ring. The stories of *The Hobbit* and *The Lord of the Rings* took place in the last century of the Third Age. That age ended with the destruction of the Ring and the final overthrow of Sauron, but the Fourth Age, the age of the dominion of man, was held to have begun only when the Guardians of the Elven Rings left Middle-earth for the Undying Lands.

Tolkien's intention was to depict an age of the world that had passed, leaving only vague but evocative memories, before our recorded history began. However, rather than making that age remote and alien, he gave the major cultures of Middle-earth a flavor at once pagan and chivalrous. Even a few relative modernities have intruded, so that Tolkien's Middle-earth is a world belonging to no time, but having an internal time that is completely consistent.

The concern with chronologies in Tolkien's works first occurred early in *The Hobbit* — the Dwarves' quest could only be achieved on Durin's Day when the last moon of autumn and the sun were in the sky at the same time. The occurrence of that event could no longer be predicted by the Dwarves; throughout the story there was an urgency to arrive at Erebor in time for the last moon of autumn, coupled with concern that the next Durin's Day might still be years off.

The chronology of *The Lord of the Rings* is painstakingly consistent. The sun and stars rise at times appropriate to the season, the moon waxes and wanes and rises with complete regularity. Furthermore, the sense of the passage of time is dealt with in such a way that the reader has the impression of experiencing the same duration of time that the travelers do. This is particularly noticeable when a single paragraph summarizes the activities of several days but gives the illusion that the experiences of those days have been set forth in detail.

Tolkien developed the importance of chronologies and calendars throughout the story. Just as he used differences in languages to indicate differences in peoples, he used the differing methods of reckoning time between men and Elves to indicate their differing outlooks on time. Men reckoned time in twelve-month solar years. The Elves, as immortals, saw the solar years pass too quickly — their basic unit of time was the long-year of 144 solar years. The Elves' solar-year calendar was based on the growth cycles of vegetation, and they named their six seasons for stages in the growth of plants.

With typical attention to detail, Tolkien provides a detailed Shire calendar complete with day, month, and holiday names — even the differences between the calendars of the Shire and Bree are noted. The month names, neither true Westron nor our modern Latin names, are the month names used by the Anglo-Saxons. These names are given, not in their original forms, but modified as they would have been by the changes of English if they had been retained into modern times. The Shire weekday names are an even more audacious form of word-play: Quenya *Alduya*, meaning "Treesday," becomes Trewsday in the Shire, followed by Heavensday (Hensday) and Seaday (Mersday).

Calendric systems often have mythic associations — for example, our English weekday names honor Teutonic gods. The calendars of Middle-earth are no exception. The Elvish weekday names indicate the Elves' reverence for the heavenly bodies, the Blessed Realm, and the Valar. The Shire calendar, with its intercalary *lithes* and *yules* at the solstices, recalls the ancient Egyptian calendar which also had five intercalary days. The Egyptians attributed their intercalary days to Thoth, who won them from the moon so that the goddess Nut could have her five divine children outside the existing year.

The best example of the importance of myth to Tolkien's chronologies is the emphasis placed on certain dates throughout his works. These dates include one of the old Celtic quarter-days, the solstices, and the equinoxes.

The Celtic high days divided the year into quarters, being

celebrated on or near the first of November, February, May, and August. These festivals date back to the traditions of pre-agricultural herdsmen. Today they are known as All Hallows, Candlemas, May Day, and Lammas. May first, the Celtic Cétsamain or Beltane, was celebrated with purifying fires even into Christianity. This was the date Tolkien chose for the coronation of Aragorn as King Elessar, and, later, for the marriage of Samwise to Rose Cotton.

The importance of the solstices and equinoxes developed later than that of the quarter-days, although they were still of great antiquity. These days of astronomical importance were first celebrated by agricultural peoples. Since the calendar used in the Middle-earth chronology is shifted slightly from ours, it is difficult to place the dates given accurately in the solar year. However, Tolkien stated that Midyear's Day and Yule corresponded to the solstices.

The autumnal equinox corresponds roughly to both Bilbo and Frodo's birthday, which was also the date that they rode out with the Guardians of the Elven Rings to the Grey Havens, and the date that Samwise left the Shire for the Havens some sixty years later. December twenty-fifth, our Yule but not the hobbits', was the date that the Company of the Ring left Rivendell to begin their quest. March twenty-fifth, which approximates the vernal equinox, is still celebrated as Lady Day, the Annunciation, and was the old Phrygian, Cappadocian, and Gallic celebration of the Crucifixion, was the date of the destruction of the Ring, the beginning of the new age, and, later, of the birth of Samwise's first child, Elanor. The use of these two Christian holidays (previously pagan celebrations) for the commencement and culmination of the quest underlines the ethical direction of the journey. Midyear's Day (the summer solstice and Saint John's Day) was the date Aragorn was trothplighted to Arwen and the date of their wedding nearly forty years later.

Tolkien emphasizes these traditionally significant dates paralleling the importance these days had for ancient peoples. The Celts particularly had placed the important events of their myths and legendary histories on their significant days. Several events in the Cuchulain and Fionn Cycles of Irish myth occur on the quarter-day Samhain, the eve of November when supernatural forces had the ascendancy. The turning points in the *Book of Invasions*, the mythic prehistory of Ireland, often occurred on May Eve.

P A R T
III

PLACES

PLACES

THE LANDSCAPE in which the action in myths takes place has varying roles. In some cases a myth is intended to explain the name or origin of an actual landmark. In other cases, fantastic landscapes appear in myths to challenge a hero or house a god. Often myths take place in familiar settings that either are or could be real. The latter is the case in Tolkien's Middle-earth.

The world of *The Lord of the Rings* consists of three land masses of varying levels of reality. These are Middle-earth, Númenor, and the Blessed Realm.

Middle-earth itself is a minutely mapped, geographically consistent continent that extends north, south, and east beyond knowledge, to lands "where the stars are strange." The sunken island Númenor is only remembered through its colonies, the kingdoms of the Dúnedain in Middle-earth. Although treated historically, the account of Númenor begins and ends with mythic themes. The Blessed Realm, the home of gods and immortal Elves, is a place based entirely on myth. Farther removed than even drowned Númenor, the Blessed Realm was displaced by divine power "from the circles of the world."

*

6

Middle-earth

By MIDDLE-EARTH, Tolkien meant the same area that was called *Midgard* in Old Norse, *middangeard* in Old English, and in Middle English *middelerd* or *meddelearth*.[1] It is central in that it is sandwiched between heaven and Hel and bounded by unknown lands and seas on all points of the compass.

The question often arises as to how closely the world of Middle-earth corresponds to Europe. As will be described, the correspondence is sufficient to indicate that if Tolkien was not making a positive identification, European geography was at any rate at the back of his mind. This identification explains why Middle-earth seems to pre-exist the plot of *The Lord of the Rings,* rather than the geographical features having been devised to supply obstacles and adventures for the characters, as seemed to be the case in the less fully developed world of *The Hobbit.*

There are certainly great discrepancies between the maps of Middle-earth and of Europe, but this is as it should be. It is futile and ultimately disappointing to attempt to make a one-to-one correspondence between fantasy and reality. Furthermore, Tolkien supposed the world to have changed since the

---

[1] Jakob Grimm, *Teutonic Mythology,* vol. II, p. 794.

time of the Ring, and intended the maps to be taken as the work of hobbits, who could not be expected to be expert cartographers.

Placing the European and Middle-earth maps side by side, one may make numerous comparisons. Starting in the north, the Ice Bay of Forochel is like Lübecker Bay on the Baltic Sea, the Gulf of Lune might be the mouth of the Seine, and the Greyflood, the Loire. The Misty Mountains could be the Ardennes or Les Cevénnes, while the Anduin resembles the complex of the Rhine and the Rhone. The latter forms a many-mouthed delta like the Ethir Anduin.

The Iberian Peninsula is represented only by the vestigial Cape of Andrast. The Pyrenees appear as the Ered Nimrais, the White Mountains, while the Ephel Duath and Ered Lithui ring Mordor in the same way that the Alps encircle the Po Valley. The inland sea of Mordor, the Bitter Sea of Nurnen, is bitter for the good reason that it corresponds to the Adriatic arm of the Mediterranean Sea.

Umbar could be the Bay of Naples or even the Bay of Tunis. Dol Amroth might represent the city of Cadiz, which the ancients called Gades; Minas Tirith resembles Lyon, while Pelargir suggests the city of Arles, which the Romans knew as Arelete. On the very edge of the known world eastward, the Sea of Rhûn, fed by the Celduin and the Carnen, is comparable to the Black Sea with the Danube and the Drava.

Tolkien's use of an entire continent with all its geological complexity as the background for his works provides these books with an unusual scope. In imaginative fiction, and particularly science fiction, it is common for the action to take place in one specific type of environment, for example, a desert or ice-age world. This device provides a laboratory-like situation for examining the behavior of man. However, the device seems unrealistic to us as inhabitants of a world whose environmental variety is well-known. Tolkien's use of this variety goes far toward producing a convincing setting for his story.

Tolkien had an intense love of the natural world. He expressed this immediately when he introduced the Shire in *The Hobbit* as existing ". . . long ago in the quiet of the world when there was less noise and more green . . ." This love is demonstrated by the clarity of his descriptions of landscapes. At no time are these landscapes supernatural or impossible, but the vividness with which they are depicted is essential to the appeal of Tolkien's works. He put this simply himself: " 'The green earth, say you? That is a mighty matter of legend, though you tread it under the light of day!' "[2]

[2] J. R. R. Tolkien, *The Two Towers*, p. 37.

7

Númenor

THE HISTORY of Númenor began with the war between the Elves and Morgoth, the Great Enemy. The Edain fought in this war allied with the Elves. At the war's end, the Valar, the Guardians of the World, rewarded the Edain with two gifts: long life-spans for themselves and their descendants, and the island Elenna lying west of Middle-earth.

The Edain renamed the island Númenor, which means "Land of the West" in Quenya. Dúnedain, the name the Númenoreans took for themselves in Sindarin, means "Men of the West." In the Common Speech, Númenor was referred to as Westernesse.

At first the Númenoreans retained their allegiance to the Blessed Realm and worshiped the Valar. Later generations became covetous of the Undying Lands and, at the instigation of Sauron, set out in a fleet of war to take the Blessed Realm by force. As the Númenorean king, Ar-Pharazôn the Golden, set foot upon the shore, the Valar called upon the One to protect their land. As a result, the Blessed Realm was removed beyond the circles of the earth forever, and Númenor sank beneath a vast wave. Only nine ships containing Elendil and his followers, still faithful to the Valar, escaped to Middle-earth. There Elendil founded the kingdoms of Arnor and Gondor.[1]

The story of Númenor begins and ends with mythic themes. After a war with an evil divinity, the story begins when Elros, son of Eärendil the Morning Star, led his people to a divinely appointed new land. Such foundings of lands by divinely or mysteriously born heroes are common in myth: the cases of Romulus and Remus, Abraham, and Moses, are comparable. Incredible longevity such as that of the Dúnedain is often ascribed to ancestral heroes and peoples, as can be seen throughout the Book of Genesis.

Númenor's end is comparable to the innumerable myths of deluges and land subsidences which occur to punish a land's sinful inhabitants or to herald a new age. The story of Númenor, like the Biblical account of the Deluge, serves both purposes.

The idea that large areas of inhabited land could be instantly destroyed, whether by divine punishment or nature's whim, is a powerful one. It reflects the mythic emphasis on the uncertainty of life and the subordination of man to the forces of nature. Several stories of drowned cities and lands end with the admonitory assurance that the ruins can still be seen when the water is low, or that bells in drowned towers can still be heard ringing in the tide.

Legends of drowned lands are common in medieval literature. The Celts had several stories about drowned cities, such as the tradition that an ancient British town called Caer Arianrhod once stood near Clynnog in Caernarvonshire. It was swallowed by the sea but its ruins were supposed to be visible at the neap tide.[2] Medieval writers also had traditions

[1] J. R. R. Tolkien, *The Return of the King*, p. 317.
[2] *The Mabinogion*, p. 301.

of mythical western islands similar to Númenor. These included St. Brendan's Island west of Ireland, the island Brazil for which the South American country was named, the lost Breton city of Is, and Isle Verte which still appeared on maps as late as 1853.

The story of Númenor is most similar to that of Atlantis. Atlantis was reputed to be a large land mass. Beyond it lay smaller islands, like the islands of the Blessed Realm that lay west of Númenor.

The ony known ancient references to Atlantis were made by Plato. It is unknown whether he had a source for his description or invented the story. According to Plato's account in *Timaeus*,[3] Egyptian priests conversing with the Athenian statesman Solon described a vast island called Atlantis that had lain beyond the Pillars of Hercules. This island had been as large as Asia Minor and Libya combined, and an archipelago of lesser islands had lain beyond it. Nine thousand years before Solon's birth, Atlantis had been ruled by a powerful kingdom. This had overrun almost the entire Mediterranean area; Athens alone had resisted it. The island had finally subsided, but shoals and mud flats remained visible where it had been.

Not only the geography, location, and drowning of Númenor resemble those of Atlantis, but their histories of conquest are similar. The Númenorean kings established an empire along the western coasts of Middle-earth, subdued Sauron, and were defeated only when they assaulted the Blessed Realm.

Tolkien's choice of mythic themes for the story of Númenor makes the account seem less like a history than like a myth of

[3] Plato, *The Works of Plato*, vol. IV, p. 372.

origin. The supernatural beginning and ending provide a mystical glory for the origin of the northern and southern Dúnedain, suggesting that they were chosen and guided by the Valar throughout their history.

8

The Blessed Realm

LITTLE IS TOLD about the Blessed Realm except in Bilbo's song about Eärendil and Tolkien's notes in *The Road Goes Ever On*. The Blessed Realm was isolated from Middle-earth both by the sea and by Evernight, a barrier of darkness between the mortal and immortal lands, that had been laid on the sea by Varda, the Queen of the Valar.

The Blessed Realm consisted of Eressëa ("The Lonely Isle") and the larger land mass of Valinor ("The Land of the Valar"). Eressëa lay just off the east coast of Valinor. Elves lived both on the Lonely Isle and the eastern coasts of Valinor, so both areas were given the name Eldamar ("Elvenhome"). The city of Eldamar was called Tirion and lay beside the Shadowmere.

Valinor was protected by the Pelori ("Encircling Mountains"). To the east, these mountains were pierced by the Calacirya ("Light Cleft"), a ravine through which the light of the Two Trees had issued into the coastlands. Valimar ("the City of the Valar") lay within the Encircling Mountains, near the mound where the Two Trees stood. By the time Eärendil sailed to the Blessed Realm, the trees had been destroyed by Morgoth and twilight lay on the lands they once had illuminated.

The tallest of the Encircling Mountains was also the tallest mountain in the world, Taniquetil ("High White Peak"). This mountain, called Oiolosse or Uilos ("Everwhite"), bore the domed halls of Varda (Elbereth) and of Manwe, the Elder King.[1]

Blessed western islands, the abode of immortals or departed spirits, form a common theme in myth. People concerned with the daily cycle of the sun associated the west not only with death, but also with immortality, for from the west the sun continued its apparent subterranean journey to its rising in the east.

Many civilizations have considered the west to contain the immortal land. To the Sumerians it was the western island paradise, Dilmun, where the wolf and the lamb are no longer enemies and there is no old age. To the Egyptians, it was the mountains westward in Libya. To the Greeks it was various semimythical western islands. To the Teutons, it seemed that the blessed lived in the British Isles, while the British peoples saw Ireland as the immortal land.

The Irish themselves looked westward to the land of the dead, associating it with a small, rocky island called Tech Duinn ("the House of Donn"), to which Donn, mythical ancestor of the Irish, invited the dead. Beyond this was a mythical archipelago of "three times fifty distant isles" where there was no decay or death, but, instead, innocent love, feasting, and music of unearthly beauty. In the seventh-century Irish poem "The Voyage of Bran," a beautiful elvish woman bearing a silver branch of apple blossoms described this other-world of islands to Bran. One stanza of her song is particularly

[1] Tolkien, *The Fellowship of the Ring*, p. 247; Tolkien and Swann, *The Road Goes Ever On*, p. 61.

reminiscent of Tolkien's description of the jeweled sands over which Eärendil came to Elvenhome:

> Then if one sees the Silvery Land
> on which dragonstones and crystal rain
> the sea breaks the wave upon the land
> with crystal tresses from its mane . . .[2]

Tolkien's nebulous description of Eldamar and Valinor is in accordance with Celtic usage, which has several different views of the afterlife and the otherworld. In some the dead lived apart from other beings, as in the House of Donn. Some otherworlds were the dwelling only of elvish folk; in others the dead lived among and were ruled by elvish peoples. By reason of their immortality, the Celtic elves and old gods could come and go from the otherworld with no ill effect. No mortal, not even a hero, could do so without facing perils, or without undergoing changes which were often fatal. This was equally true of Tolkien's Blessed Realm. Elves traveled with ease to, if not often from, Elvenhome, but only rarely were mortals accepted in the dwellings of the Valar. The disastrous reception of the proud warriors from Númenor is typical of the perilous face the otherworld showed its assailants. The doom set on Eärendil, who was sent to sail the sky as the Morning Star, demonstrates the type of transformation that could be wrought on even the few allowed to view the otherworld's secrets.

The name of the Undying Lands, Aman the Blessed, suggests the faërie Emain of the Celts. This has been identified with the Isle of Arran in the Firth of Clyde.[3] Emain was believed to be a green island of apple trees as were Avilon and

[2] MacCana, *Celtic Mythology*, p. 124.
[3] *Ibid.*, p. 73.

the western island gardens of the Hesperides from which
Hercules brought the apples of gold.

The closing of *The Return of the King*, in which Frodo,
Bilbo, Gandalf, Galadriel, Elrond, and other Elves sailed to the
Blessed Realm, has a close parallel in *Le Morte Darthur*. At
the end of Malory's work, a barge of fair women and a queen
all dressed in black came to the mortally wounded King
Arthur and bore him away. He told his companion, Sir
Bedevere, that he was going to the Vale of Avilon for healing.
There was a question whether he was buried in a chapel that
night, or lived on, or would live again.[4] The parallel to this
mystical sequence, the scene at the Grey Havens, is comparably ambiguous in differentiating between immortality and
death.

[4] Malory, *Le Morte Darthur*, vol. II, p. 491.

P A R T
IV

BEINGS

BEINGS

THE LIVING BEINGS of Middle-earth are as various as the lands they inhabit. There are over thirty-five types of mortals, immortals, and monsters mentioned in Tolkien's works, besides a wide selection of animal life that plays a lesser part.

Most of these beings are derived to some extent from mythology. Men play much the same sort of part in Tolkien's works as they do in myths and legends, as do Elves, Dwarves, Wizards, and other major types of characters. Even some of the most obscure have origins in old lore. The Variags of Khand, for example, mentioned only twice, derive their name from that of the Varyags, ancient Scandinavian warriors.

However, the most important characters, the hobbits, from whose viewpoint the War of the Ring and the events leading up to it are seen, are Tolkien's individual idea. It is this blending of the traditional with the imaginative that places Tolkien's works in the unusual literary position that they occupy.

The natures of the peoples in Tolkien's works, their relationships and their motivations, are complex. In almost all cases the impression is given that Tolkien has told much less than he knew about the peoples in question, rather than producing spear-carriers to fill in background space.

The fact that the lesser peoples have any motivations at all is laudable for imaginative fiction. The enemies are not simply unreasonably evil. The Orcs, Trolls, and the Balrog were created evil by an evil power. They were made for a purpose and did not have the will to question their way of life. As for the men, those who were wholly enemies were so for a cause: lost land to regain, cities to protect, or empires to establish. The others, such as the Southrons shot down in Ithilien, fought for the forces that bribed or threatened them.

Good or ill, all the characters have a depth. They do not exist only to provide an aid or obstacle for the protagonists, but have some comprehensible reason behind their action. Even the most incongruous and inhuman creature, the giant spider Shelob, had her own motivation: insane and monstrous as it was, it is an obsession that can be understood.

For the purposes of this book, the beings are separated into three main divisions: hobbits, men, and Old Gods. The section on hobbits also includes the hobbits' curious relative, Sméagol-Gollum. The section on men contains the groups and characters most interesting from a mythological point of view from the three divisions of men in Middle-earth: the High, the Middle, and the Wild. The section called "The Old Gods" contains the immortal, supernatural, and mythical peoples derived from the divinities of ancient myth. This section includes the Valar, Wizards, Elves, Dwarves, Bombadil, Ents, and such evil beings as Sauron, the Nazgûl, and the Balrog.

9

Hobbits

THE HOBBITS hold a unique position among the peoples of *The Lord of the Rings*. They are Tolkien's individual idea rather than a people out of mythology, and they live by a set of very human ideals in contrast to the glorified lives of the Wise, the Elves, and the Dúnedain.

The hobbits have the universal appeal of little things. They live a simple, satisfying provincial life close to the land. They are self-indulgent, childlike, but self-sufficient. Their power lies in an unexpected ability to withstand evil.

The human nature of the hobbits is far more evident than that of the heroic men in the story. The hobbit viewpoint maintains a humble, human, familiar tone in a story that would otherwise be sonorous, serious, and unapproachable.

Hobbits become heroes unexpectedly, and for this reason are all the more appealing. Fate chooses the hobbits rather than choosing the wise or powerful, and the hobbits accept the role, surprised that they do so. On the whole, Frodo's heroism was not in valiant deeds such as his cousin Bilbo's, or even those of Samwise. His heroism lay in the acceptance of an almost impossible task, the endurance to continue in the face of unexpected obstacles, and the ability to resist the power and temptation of the Ring.

Perhaps it is because hobbits are not part of the mythic milieu that neither Bilbo nor Frodo entirely completed their quests. Bilbo confronted the dragon and gathered the information needed to overcome it, but, not unexpectedly, did not kill it himself. Frodo, after struggling with the Ring to the brink of Doom, was unable to take the final necessary action of consigning it to the flames.

Although the hobbits are not the creatures of myth, mythology enters into the stories about them. Bilbo Baggins' confrontation of the dragon in the Lonely Mountain and the subsequent events of *The Hobbit* closely follow the story line of the dragon sequence in *Beowulf*, an incongruous and conscious parallel which must not have been lost on Tolkien's scholarly colleagues.

In *Beowulf*, a fugitive thrall in search of a hiding place crept into an underground lair and discovered a sleeping dragon guarding a vast, ancient treasure. In spite of his fear of the monster, the slave stole a jeweled cup with which to buy his master's pardon. The dragon discovered his loss immediately and, unable to catch the thief, spent the night in killing and burning in the surrounding land, even destroying Beowulf's royal hall. Although an old man, Beowulf set out with a small party to destroy the dragon. In an awesome battle, Beowulf stabbed the dragon to death, but not before it wounded him fatally with its venomous fangs.

Comparable in the stories of Beowulf and Bilbo are the guarding of a golden hoard by a dragon underground, the theft of a precious cup by an undistinguished person, and the dragon's immediate recognition that a single item was missing from a vast treasury. In both tales the thief escaped and the raging dragon caused destruction that brought about his doom. The dragon was killed in both cases and in both a hero died.

Tolkien's treatment of the story is distinguished by his sense of justice. Tolkien's dragon deserved to be robbed: the Dwarves were only attempting to regain their ancestral treasure. For that reason too, the Dwarves and Bilbo deserved their escape. The dragon's death was just: his attack on Lake-town was unprovoked. For killing the dragon, Bard, instead of suffering Beowulf's heroic death, became Lord of Dale. Thorin Oakenshield, as the hero who died, brought his fate upon himself because he was uncompromising about the distribution of the hoard. However, on his deathbed he saw his errors and forgave Bilbo for going against his will.

Another mythic characteristic in the story of the hobbits is the name Frodo itself, which comes from Teutonic tradition. It is probably derived from Frô, a form of the name of the Scandinavian fertility god, Frey. The name seems to mean "wise" or "fruitful" and appears in *Beowulf* in the form Froda. Frodo and the legendary King Fródi of Denmark, another namesake of Frey, both show evidence of increasing the fertility of their lands in the tradition of the god. The year 1420 (Shire Reckoning), after Frodo's return to and cleansing of the Shire, was a period remarkable for its bountiful crops, good health, and plentiful births and marriages. In Denmark, the reign of Fródi, a descendant of Odin, was also a time of abundance. Fródi brought this about by using two magic millstones which ground out whatever he desired. Fródi had them grind out gold, peace, and prosperity. For this reason gold had the kenning "Fródi's flour."

The most important mythic theme concerning the hobbits was the escape from death made by Frodo, Bilbo, and Samwise to the Undying Lands. This escape satisfies the universal wish for eternal life, but is tempered by eternal separation from the world. Perhaps the most poignant element of the journey to the Blessed Realm is that the reader recognizes it, when it occurs, as foredoomed. Frodo had dreamed of the journey in the house of Bombadil, and had been unconsciously and inexorably moving toward it ever since.

10

Sméagol-Gollum

SMÉAGOL was a descendant of the Stoors, one of the three branches of hobbit-kind. The hobbits originated in the Anduin River Valley. They gradually migrated westward, as Greenwood the Great came under the Necromancer's spell and began to be called Mirkwood. After the hobbits had settled in the lands west of the Misty Mountains, the wars between the Dúnedain and the Witch-king drove many of the Stoors back to the Anduin. There they developed into a folk who lived in burrows along the riverside, and were not too different from their relatives in the Shire and Bree.

The only noteworthy member of this pleasant tribe was the uncharacteristic Sméagol. His name, appropriately, means "burrowing, worming in" in the Old English used to translate the language of the men of Wilderland. He was constantly obsessed with origins and sources and spent his time delving and diving in search of secrets. However, it was his friend Déagol ("secret") who happened upon the One Ring in the Anduin bed 2461 years[1] after it had been lost there by Isildur. The power of the Ring brought Déagol to grief as soon as he had found it: since he would not relinquish it, Sméagol murdered him for the precious gold.

[1] Tolkien, *The Return of the King*, pp. 366–368.

Sméagol used the Ring for spying and malice throughout his extensive family until he was disowned by the matriarch, his grandmother. In his subsequent wanderings, Sméagol developed a hatred of the sun and moon. As a spying, sneaking creature himself, he pictured the sun and moon as all-seeing celestial eyes that spied out his every action. To elude these eyes and to search again for secrets, Sméagol crept into the orc-tunnels under the Misty Mountains. With his life prolonged by the Ring, but too resilient to become a wraith under its power, he lived on an island in a subterranean pool for 471 years until discovered by Bilbo Baggins.

After he lost the Ring to Bilbo, Sméagol emerged and searched Wilderland for it, first retracing Bilbo's travels and then turning south toward the power in Mordor. Eventually, traveling in the moonless hours of night, he reached the Ephel Dúath mountains on the border of the Black Country. There, with hatred and fear, he worshiped Shelob in her loathsome tunnels. He entered Mordor, and was captured, questioned, and released by Sauron. He was captured in the Dead Marshes by Aragorn, questioned by Gandalf, and placed in the Wood-elves' guardianship. He escaped from the Elves with the aid of raiding Orcs, and finally made his way to Moria. From Moria he followed the Company of the Ring to the Emyn Muil where Frodo and Sam captured him.

At this time, another symptom of his madness resurfaced in the form of a divided personality, one part professing to a respect for the hobbits' mercy and a desire to aid them, the other part obsessed with desire for the Ring. Reluctantly, the hobbits accepted him as their guide. Treacherously, he left them to die in Shelob's Lair. When they escaped, he followed them through Mordor to Mount Doom. There the Ring overpowered him and he became the agent of the Ring's destruction. The irony of his death is that after a lifelong obsession with origins and secrets for which he searched vainly underground, he died in the subterranean forging-place of the One Ring, the single secret of his life.

Among mythological creatures, Sméagol is most comparable to the Dwarf Andvari of Scandinavian legend. Like Sméagol, Andvari was the guardian of a precious ring of doom. He was a Dwarf who usually took the form of a pike, a combination of small man and water-creature comparable to the small, web-footed Gollum. Andvari lived under a waterfall and was caught there by the god Loki. Loki wanted the Dwarf's treasure as a weregild to pay his host, whose son he had accidentally killed. Andvari relinquished all his hoard except the ring, which he tried to conceal. When it too was taken, he cursed it to bring tragedy on all its owners.[2] It is likely that Tolkien's vivid and sympathetic psychological study of Gollum arises from his analysis of such a half-human water-creature as Andvari, who lived a solitary and lightless life hoarding a precious but destructive secret.

Some other characteristics of Sméagol's are reminiscent of such goblins as the Teutonic Goldemar, also called Vallmar. Goldemar, like Gollum with his Ring, was invisible: only his shadow could be seen, like the shadow of the Ring-bearer. Goldemar was described as small and froglike, and, again like the ever-hungry Gollum, as a cannibal. When a curious mortal tried to trace the invisible goblin by strewing ashes that would show his footprints, the angry Goldemar caught and ate him.[3]

Goldemar seems to have been an example of a common enough type of malicious sprite, but his invisibility with a visible shadow may have been one of the inspirations for Tolkien's description of the effect of the Ring.

[2] Snorri Sturluson, *The Prose Edda*, p. 112.
[3] Grimm, *Teutonic Mythology*, vol. II, p. 508.

II

Men

THE HUMANS in *The Lord of the Rings* were portrayed as a people coming into their own. Their age was approaching, while that of the supernatural peoples was receding.

The men of Middle-earth were classified in three divisions: the High, the Middle, and the Wild. The High were the Men of the West, the Dúnedain, descended from the Númenoreans whose ancestors aided the Elves in their struggle against Morgoth. The Middle Peoples were also called the Men of Twilight. They included the Rohirrim, the Men of Bree, and the frontiersmen of Wilderland, virtuous folk, but of less high lineage and learning than the Dúnedain of Arnor and Gondor. The Wild Peoples were the Men of Darkness. Among them were the evil Easterlings, Southrons, and Men of Mordor, the manipulated Dunlendings, the spell-doomed Dead, and the untamed but faithful Woses.

THE DÚNEDAIN

The Dunedain are descendants of the Númenoreans, who in turn were descendants of the Edain. At the beginning of the Second Age of Middle-earth, the Valar, the Guardians of the

World, rewarded the Edain ("the Fathers of Men") for their part in the war against Morgoth by giving them the island Elenna, west of Middle-earth. Many of the Edain, who had been widespread in the north, migrated to Elenna in the year 32. They renamed the island Númenor, or Westernesse, and called themselves Númenoreans.

In the year 600 of the Second Age, the Númenoreans, desiring trade and empire, began to return to Middle-earth. They started to set up harbors along the western coasts in the year 1200, and permanent colonies around 1800.

In the year 2251, dissension arose among the Númenoreans. The majority became dissatisfied that the Valar had only granted them long life-spans, and began to desire immortality as well. A minority remained faithful in their reverence of the Valar. In 3319, Sauron encouraged the disloyal Númenoreans to attack the Valar and attempt to obtain immortality by force. Númenor was overwhelmed by the sea by divine command, and only the faithful Númenoreans escaped. They were driven by a storm to the southwestern coast of Middle-earth. In the following year their leader, Elendil, established the North Kingdom, Arnor ("Royal Land"), and the South Kingdom, Gondor ("Land of Stone"). He ruled these two kingdoms with the aid of his sons Isildur and Anárion until he was killed during the conquest of Sauron, which ended the Second Age in the year 3441. Arnor and Gondor remained monarchies for about two thousand years.

In Gondor, the last king had no descendants. The government was thereafter administered by hereditary Ruling Stewards descended from the line of the kings' stewards. The people of Gondor retained the noble traditions of Númenor. They were the primary defenders of the West against the power of Mordor.

In Arnor, the descendants of the last king became hereditary Chieftains of the northern Dúnedain, who became a people of the wilderness and were called Rangers. They were wood-wise and knew the speech of bird and beast, but kept the traditions of Númenor. They retained the gift that had been given to the Númenoreans of a long life, even longer than that of the Dúnedain of the south, whose lineage was not as pure. Although distrusted by such settled people as the Breelanders, the Rangers were the secret guardians of the north and had the friendship of Elrond and the Elves in Rivendell.

Pivotal characters among the Dúnedain were the Ranger Aragorn of Arnor; Denethor, the last Ruling Steward of Gondor, and his sons, Boromir and Faramir.

ARAGORN

Aragorn is a particularly complex character. He first appeared in *The Fellowship of the Ring* climbing over the Bree gate in an unquestionably suspicious manner. He evolved in presence and nobility until he was crowned King Elessar of Arnor and Gondor.

Aragorn typifies the myth-hero. A wide variety of heroes in mythology have a number of incidents in common in their stories, probably because people universally need to believe in the capacity to achieve certain fundamental goals. These achievements were given supernatural form in heroic myth.

Twenty-two such common points in the stories of heroes were listed by Lord Raglan in his book *The Hero*.[1] The myths that Raglan drew from include those of Sigurd, King

[1] Raglan, *The Hero*, pp. 174–175.

Arthur, Perseus, and Moses. The list of points is not exhaustive, but is generally representative. Significantly, most of the points enumerated by Raglan are included in the story of Aragorn, as will be shown.

Raglan's outline is as follows:

1. The hero's mother is a royal virgin.
2. His father is king and
3. Often a near relative of his mother, but
4. The circumstances of his conception are unusual, and
5. He is also reputed to be the son of a god.
6. At birth, an attempt is made, usually by his father or maternal grandfather, to kill him, but,
7. He is spirited away, and
8. Reared by foster parents in a far country.
9. We are told nothing of his childhood, but
10. On reaching manhood he returns or goes to his future kingdom.
11. After a victory over the king and/or a giant, dragon or wild beast
12. He marries a princess, often the daughter of his predecessor, and
13. Becomes king.
14. For a time he rules uneventfully, and
15. Prescribes laws, but
16. Later he loses favor with the gods and/or his subjects,
17. Is driven from the throne and city, after which
18. He meets with a mysterious death
19. Often on top of a hill.
20. His children, if any, do not succeed him.
21. His body is not buried, but nevertheless,
22. He has one or more holy sepulchers.

This pattern is closely reflected in the story of Aragorn, especially as told in Appendix A of *The Return of the King*.[2] The correlation is not accidental. Tolkien was familiar with heroic myths from a variety of cultures and he selected from them the elements that he felt typified the hero. To conform to his concept of justice, Tolkien omitted the tragic theme from Aragorn's history, but transferred elements of tragedy to his queen, Arwen, who died in exile, although in hope of "joy beyond the walls of the world." For comparison, elements of Aragorn's story are given here with numbers corresponding to those in Raglan's list.

Aragorn's mother, Gilraen, was a descendant of the first Chieftain of the Dúnedain, Aranarth, son of Arvedui, Last King of Arnor (1). His father, Arathorn II, was fifteenth Chieftain, (2) and therefore also directly descended from Aranarth (3). Aragorn's parents were married, because of the prophecy of Ivorwen, Gilraen's mother, only four years before Arathorn's untimely death (4).

Aragorn was adopted by Elrond Halfelven, an immortal and greatest of the Wise (5), because the Enemy was seeking to slay Aragorn as the heir of Isildur (6). He was raised secretly in Rivendell (7) and given the name Estel ("Hope"), in Elrond's house (8). Nothing further is told of Aragorn until he came of age and was told his secret lineage (9). At this time he met and fell in love with Elrond's daughter Arwen, who had been living in Lórien with her grandmother, Galadriel.

Among many quests, Aragorn served as captain in Gondor, which was to become his kingdom (10), under the name Thorongil ("Eagle of the Star"). At that time he overthrew the captain of the Corsairs of Umbar. During the War of the

---

[2] Tolkien, *The Return of the King*, pp. 337, 344.

Ring he aided in the overthrow of Saruman and Sauron. He alone challenged the Dark Lord, revealing himself as heir of Isildur in the palantír of Orthanc (11).

He married Elrond's daughter, Arwen, descendant of heroes and Elven-kings (12), on Mid-year's Day, after having been crowned king on May Day (13). He reigned uneventfully (14), after pronouncing judgments at the end of the War of the Ring (15).

On March first, the same date as his birth, Aragorn died by his own will (18), in the House of the Kings on the hill of Minas Tirith (19), at the age of two hundred eight years,[3] elsewhere mentioned as one hundred ninety.[4] At the king's death, Arwen went alone from Minas Tirith to the empty forest of Lórien, where she died alone on the hill of Cerin Amroth (17). Aragorn's son, Eldarion, apparently did succeed him. Aragorn's body long lay in state unburied (21).

Of the many heroes who have comparable histories, Aragorn is most similar to King Arthur. Not only were both taken as infants to foster homes, but for the same reason: They were in danger because they were heirs to great kingdoms, and rival forces sought to destroy them. Until they took the throne, their kingdoms were kingless realms in disorder, plagued with lawlessness and violence. Upon coming of age, each obtained a famous sword with an unusual history and each unexpectedly learned his heritage.

In the cases of both Arthur and Aragorn, the claim to the throne was challenged, and it was necessary that they prove themselves worthy of the kingdom, by fulfilling a prophecy and also by engaging in battle. The two kings had comparable relationships with wise counselors who were wizards with prophetic powers and who skillfully guided their kings

[3] *Ibid.*, pp. 318, 370.
[4] *Ibid.*, p. 324.

and the kings' companions. Both kings did numerous heroic deeds, but neither was famous for one single outstanding act of heroism.

Aragorn also has similarities to Charlemagne. Each restored an ancient fallen empire. To attain the empire, each had to fight a war, west against east. Charlemagne's war was with the Lombards, who occupied a position on the map similar to that of Mordor in Middle-earth. Both wars were won when a small party slipped unnoticed through a mountain pass, outflanked the eastern army, and demoralized it.

Aragorn and Charlemagne were each crowned with a famous, ancient crown by the spiritual leader of their world, Charlemagne by Pope Leo III.

Aragorn is reminiscent of the non-historical Charlemagne as well. A cycle of romances like those that are told about King Arthur also grew up around Charlemagne and were later applied to Charles V, Frederic Barbarossa, and other national leaders. In these romances, Charlemagne's loved one was an elf-woman,[5] as Aragorn's was the Elven Arwen.

Charlemagne, like Aragorn with the *athelas*, cured people with a special herb. During a pestilence, Charlemagne was said to have had a dream in which an angel told him to shoot an arrow and use whatever herb it struck to heal the plague. When he woke, he shot an arrow which struck a sowthistle, so he used this herb in healing the sick.[6]

In the romances it is said that when Frederic Barbarossa returns to the world, he will hang his shield on a withered tree, it will break into leaf, and a better time will come.[7] This is comparable to Aragorn's planting of the new White

[5] Grimm, *Teutonic Mythology*, vol. III, p. xlvi.
[6] *Ibid.*, p. 1208.
[7] *Ibid.*, p. 955.

Tree in the place of the Dead Tree at the beginning of a new age.

Tolkien added a number of other mythic elements to Aragorn's story, enhancing his noble, heroic, and supernatural qualities. Some of these themes are relatively obscure while others are widely represented. They are given here in the order of their appearance in *The Lord of the Rings*.

One theme which occurs in Aragorn's story is so widespread and significant that Raglan could well have included it in his list. This is the theme of the hero's descent into and return from the underworld. This journey was undertaken by such heroes as Hercules, Odysseus, Orpheus, Theseus, Aeneas, King Arthur, Odin, Hermod, and Vainamoinen. Aragorn's quest was a comparable one when he followed the Paths of the Dead, tunnels from which no man had returned living. Aragorn emerged again into the living world leading the Dead, and, as had been prophesied, the Dead swore allegiance to him for the War of the Ring.

Aragorn was described as wearing certain tokens which have a mythic significance. These were the Star of the North Kingdom, the Elven Cloak, and the Elfstone from Lórien.

Aragorn wore the Star of the North Kingdom, the diamond Elendilmir, on his brow as a sign of royalty when he sailed up the Anduin to Minas Tirith. This star is reminiscent of the stars on the foreheads of heroes in the Märchen[8] and in Tolkien's *Smith of Wootton Major*.[9] In the latter cases, the stars were not simply worn, but appeared supernaturally, singling the bearer out for an unusual fate.

The grey Elven cloak used by Aragorn to disguise himself

[8] *Ibid.*, vol. I, p. 391.
[9] Tolkien, *Smith of Wootton Major*, p. 22.

after the Battle of Pelennor Field is similar to several dis-
guising cloaks in myth. In an Irish tale, the hero Curoi wore
a cloak so that he was known only as "the man in the grey
mantle."[10] In the same way, Aragorn, unrecognized, was
referred to as "one cloaked in grey." Sir Gromer, in the
Arthurian poem "The Turk and Gawain," was enchanted in
the form of a Turk, a transformation that Loomis identified
with Curoi's disguise. The Turk's mantle was described as
"invisible grey,"[11] an apt description of Aragorn's camouflag-
ing cloak from Lórien. The Elven cloak may also be identified with a number of mythical cloaks of invisibility, although
it only hid the wearer, not making him truly invisible as did
the Ring.

A traditional theme which has a significant place in Aragorn's Elf-stone brooch from Lórien was so characteristic of him that the people of Minas Tirith called him Elfstone,
the name that had been prophesied for him at his birth. When
Aragorn became king, he took the name Elfstone in the High-
elven form, Elessar, as his royal name. This name is a traditional one, appearing in noble English and German families in
the forms Elphinstone and Elbenstein.

A traditional theme which has a significant place in Aragorn's story is that of the healing powers of royalty. Aragorn
established his healing faculty early, when he helped heal
Frodo's knife wound on Weathertop. He also healed both
Frodo and Samwise after they had been wounded by Orcs
in Moria. He was recognized as king after the Battle of
Pelennor Field when he healed the wounded, including those
overwhelmed by the Black Breath of the Nazgûl, thus fulfilling a prophecy in the folklore of Gondor and establishing his
royalty.

10 Loomis, *Celtic Myth and Arthurian Romance*, p. 12.
11 *Ibid.*, p. 101.

Belief in the healing powers of royalty is widespread. English kings were thought to heal scrofula by touch, so the
disease was called the King's Evil. Queen Elizabeth and
Charles the First were acclaimed for their healing powers.
Charles the Second touched nearly one hundred thousand
sufferers from scrofula during his reign. The English monarchs were believed to have inherited the gift from Edward
the Confessor. The French kings were said to derive their
power from Clovis or from Saint Louis.[12] In the Middle
Ages when Waldemar I, King of Denmark, traveled in
Germany, mothers brought infants and farmers brought seed
grain for him to lay his hands on, expecting both to thrive
the better for the royal touch.[13]

Several features of Aragorn's attainment of the kingship
have parallels in myth, particularly in Celtic traditions. From
very early times specific rituals accompanied the attainment
of kingdoms, rituals which were codified in myth even when
their sources were forgotten. Tolkien's development of these
elements attests to his careful attention to and selection from
the old lore.

Before Aragorn's coronation, he, Éomer, and Imrahil were
seated on thrones of turves in the Field of Cormallen. This
apparently humble honor is actually significant. Such a throne
appears in the Irish Cuchulain Cycle. When the Ulstermen
came to fight the armies of Queen Maeve, they gathered on
Slieve Sleamhain. On the highest point of the hill they made
a seat of sods and earth for Conchubar, High King of Ulster.[14]
The importance of such thrones may be seen in the Teutonic
tradition in which earth grown over with grass had a sacred

[12] Frazer, *The Golden Bough*, p. 103.
[13] *Ibid.*, p. 103.
[14] Gregory, *Cuchulain of Muirthemne*, p. 198.

power and was used in oath-taking. Also, in grasping a turf, one signified that he was taking possession of land.[15]

In ancient Ireland, the kingship and the public well-being were considered synonymous, and the qualities of the rightful king were reflected in the condition of the kingdom. If peace, justice, security, and prosperity were not maintained, the ruler was considered unfit.[16] In these terms it was necessary for Aragorn to prove himself to obtain his kingdom. Among the factors that proved his worth were his aid in the destruction of Mordor, his possession of healing power, and his dispensation of justice.

In Ireland too, the king wedded the sovereignty of the land symbolically in the person of the queen. In myths, the king wedded the national goddess, but even mortal queens were viewed as embodying the sovereignty of Ireland.[17] This may explain why Elessar held his kingship to be incomplete while he awaited the arrival of Arwen, and why she was depicted as so superior to him in majesty and lineage.

In early or primitive cultures as a widespread precaution, to prevent the downfall of the realm embodied in the king, the king had to be prevented from reigning or even living while enfeebled by sickness or old age. By dying while still hale, sometimes as a ritual sacrifice, the king transferred his soul, while still in its prime, to his successor, and so prevented the country from withering while his strength failed.[18] This tradition is exemplified by the mysterious deaths of many kings and heroes in myth which seem to indicate ritual killing. Aragorn's self-willed death seems to be in the same tradition.

[15] Grimm, vol. II, p. 642.
[16] MacCana, *Celtic Mythology*, p. 119.
[17] *Ibid.*, p. 120.
[18] Frazer, p. 310.

DENETHOR, BOROMIR, AND FARAMIR

Denethor was the last Ruling Steward of Gondor. Tolkien introduced him for only the last week of his life. This was enough to show the tragedy of a great man who overreached himself through the sins of pride and covetousness, to become the prey of the Enemy. His death, like Aragorn's, recalls the theme of kings who die mysterious deaths which prevent them from reigning in old age.

The ominous vision that caused Denethor's fatal despair is paralleled in myth. By the time of the War of the Ring, Denethor's pride caused him to seek wisdom from the Seeing-stone, although it was controlled by the Dark Lord's will. In the end, the stone showed him only visions which convinced him of inevitable defeat. The last of these visions was of a fleet of black-sailed Corsair ships coming up the Anduin, apparently cutting off defense from the south and attacking the city. This vision filled Denethor with such despair that he committed suicide. The black ships arrived after Denethor's death, bearing the Dúnedain led by Aragorn to aid Denethor's besieged city.

The same theme, that of foreboding ships causing a ruler's suicide although they actually carry a returning hero, is found in the Greek myth of Theseus. There the hero set out in a black-sailed ship as a sacrifice to the Cretan Minotaur. He promised the king, his father, that if he slew the monster he would change the sails to white as a signal of his homecoming. However, in his haste, the victorious hero forgot the promise. His father, seeing the ominous ship from the sea-cliffs, leaped to his death.

Like many of the rulers of Gondor, more concerned with the past than the present, Denethor married late in life. His wife, Finduilas of Dol Amroth, died young after bearing Denethor two sons, Boromir and Faramir.

The story of these two sons follows the pattern of many myths where one son is the father's favorite. In such stories one brother fails a test while the other passes it and wins a realm. In this case the test was the renunciation of the Ring, and the realm which Faramir won the princedom of Emyn Arnen in Ithilien. This theme is very widespread. It appears in different forms in the Old Testament stories of Jacob and Esau and of Joseph and his brothers, as well as in countless folk tales.

Although Faramir renounced the Ring and won a princedom, Boromir, who succumbed to the Ring's temptation, repented and underwent a mystical experience after death. The consignment of Boromir's body to the Great River, and the reappearance of the corpse in its boat wreathed with light, suggests that Boromir's repentance was accepted both by his companions and by the Guardians of the World. Having been absolved of his sin, he was assured of spiritual rest.

The sending off of a body in a boat is a very ancient practice and an evocative one. It suggests the spirit's journey to an unknown place, the journey of the sun in darkness from sunset to sunrise, and the inexorable quality of life's flow, like that of the river or the tide.

Scandinavian burials from the Bronze Age have been found in hollowed oak trunks that resembled hollowed-tree canoes. These may have typified the sun-ship bearing the privileged dead on the nighttime path of the sun to the otherworld.[1] The same parallel is given in the Icelandic word *lur*, which means both a boat made from a hollowed-out tree trunk, and a

---

[1] Davidson, *Scandinavian Mythology*, p. 23.

coffin.[2] In the Late Bronze Age, graves were often encircled with lines of stones forming the outline of a ship with a raised prow and stern. Sometimes these stone outlines reached 150 feet in length. On one, a circle cut on the prow-stone suggests that it represented a ship of the sun.[3]

Actual ships were later used in burials, or to set the body adrift. Often valuable furnishings were placed in the ship with the body, as in Boromir's case. The Scandinavian god Balder was supposed to have been burned on a pyre which was placed on a ship on land. The body of his wife, who had died of sorrow, his horse, and Odin's ring Draupnir were placed on the pyre with him.[4]

During the Viking period, the use of ships in funeral ceremonies was common. Ship burials and stone outlines of ships over graves continued to be used. One of the most famous of its kind was the Sutton Hoo ship burial in England, which contained a rich and varied hoard.[5] The account of the funeral of the Danish King Scyld in *Beowulf* is the description of a ship-funeral told with quiet dignity. Scyld's body was laid near the ship's mast. Treasure, weapons, and armor were heaped nearby. His banner was placed above his head. His subjects allowed the water to pull the ship slowly away from shore. Its destination was as unknown to them as was Scyld's birthplace: he had come to his people by sea as a foundling.[6]

The Arthurian Cycle includes several instances of boats bearing corpses down rivers, as well as the final example of the mysterious barge that came for King Arthur himself. The

2 Snorri Sturluson, *The Prose Edda*, p. 35.
3 Davidson, *Pagan Scandinavia*, p. 44.
4 Snorri Sturluson, p. 84.
5 Davidson, *Pagan Scandinavia*, p. 113.
6 *Beowulf*, 32–52.

discovery of these boats is similar to the discovery of Boromir's boat by Faramir. Like Boromir's, the boats were often unguided. The bodies, also as Boromir's appeared to his brother, were beautiful and richly arrayed.

In Malory's *Le Morte Darthur* there are three noteworthy examples of discoveries of bodies in boats: that of King Hermance, killed by treason; that of Elaine Le Blank who died of love for Sir Launcelot; and that of Percivale's sister who died to save an ailing noblewoman. The last example is the most evocative and has the feeling most like that of the finding of Boromir's body.

When Sir Percivale's sister was dying, she asked that her body be placed in a ship to go wherever it would. The discovery of this ship by Sir Launcelot was a mystical, dreamlike sequence very much like that in which Faramir discovered his brother's body. In both cases there was a feeling of being compelled to approach the boat, a profound beauty in the scene, and an uplifted emotion in the watcher.

> So when [Sir Launcelot] was asleep there came a vision unto him and said: Launcelot, arise up and take thine armour, and enter into the first ship that thou shalt find. And when he heard these words he start up and saw great clearness about him . . . and so by adventure he came by a strand, and found a ship the which was without sail or oar. And as soon as he was within the ship there he felt the most sweetness that ever he felt, and he was fulfilled with all thing that ever he thought on or desired . . . he found there a fair bed, and therein lying a gentlewoman dead, the which was Sir Percivale's sister.[7]

[7] Malory, *Le Morte Darthur*, vol. II, p. 351.

THE MIDDLE PEOPLES

The Middle Peoples or Men of Twilight were numerous in Middle-earth. They included all the peoples other than the Men of Westernesse except the evil or Wild Men. The peoples of Rhovanion or Wilderland, the lands including Mirkwood and the surrounding country, were the primary Men of Twilight to come into the stories concerning the Ring. The most important of these were the Rohirrim, the Masters of Horses (literally "Horse-lord-folk") who left Rhovanion and were given the land Rohan for their aid in battle to Gondor. The alliance between the two countries continued throughout their history.

The Woodsmen of Mirkwood and the Men of the Long Lake were other important Middle Peoples. In each of these groups single heroes stand out in the account in *The Hobbit*. One was Bard the Bowman, who shot down the destructive dragon, Smaug. The other was Beorn, the strange, forbidding "skin-changer" who could take on the form of a giant bear at will. Both of these heroes belong to particular patterns in mythology, having supernatural powers which are widespread in myths and folk tales.

THE ROHIRRIM

The Éothéod (Old English for "Horselords") were ultimately descended from the Edain and their rulers were descended from the kings of Rhovanion (Wilderland). The Éothéod first lived in the middle Anduin Valley between the Carrock and the Gladden River. This land became crowded and came

under the influence of the Necromancer in Mirkwood, so that
in the year 1977 of the Third Age, Frumgar led most of the
Éothéod to the northern reaches of the Anduin. This region
had recently become habitable after the defeat of the Witch-
king in the north. The Horselords named this land Éothéod
after themselves.

By the twenty-first century, the Éothéod had multiplied
until they again felt overcrowded. In the year 2510, Calenard
hon, a sparsely populated northern part of Gondor, was overrun by wild men and Orcs. The Steward of Gondor called
on the Éothéod for aid. They came, led by Eorl, in time to
rescue the army of Gondor and defeat the enemies that had
surrounded it. In return, the Steward Cirion granted the
Éothéod the land Calenardhon as their own. They renamed
it the Riddermark (Old English *riddena mearc*, "land of
riders"). The people of Gondor translated the name Éothéod
into the Sindarin word Rohirrim ("Horse-lord-folk") and referred to the Mark as Rohan.

Eorl became the first king of Rohan. His horse, Felaróf,
was the ancestor of the *mearas* ("horses" in Old English), the
kings' horses, of which Shadowfax was one.

Several of the details in the stories of the Rohirrim have
parallels in Teutonic mythology. Many of the names of the
kings of Rohan are titles of nobility in Old English or are
related to the names of the Teutonic gods. Eorl means Earl,
Théoden means the leader of a people, and Baldor means
lord, prince, hero, or king. Baldor is also a version of the
name of the Scandinavian god Balder, and may be related to
the word "bold."[1] Bragi and Brego, meaning "leader," are
names of the god of poetic eloquence, from whom the word

[1] Grimm, *Teutonic Mythology*, vol. I, p. 220.

"brag" is derived.[2] Wormtongue is a name for a satirical or bitter-spoken person, referring to the *orm* or serpent rather than the angleworm. Because kings were considered friends of the gods, names such as Fréawine (Friend of Frey) and Bregowine (Friend of Brego) were considered appropriate for heroes and rulers.[3]

Equally essential to the Rohirrim and the Teutons was the versatile horse. To the Rohirrim, horses were the gift of the gods, brought to Middle-earth by Béma, the Huntsman of the Valar from the Uttermost West. The horse gave the Rohirrim their name, "Masters of Horses," and was valued next to human kin. In Teutonic mythology, the horse was considered sacred to Frey. In Celtic mythology, horses were associated with the goddess Epona. Teutonic warriors so valued their horses that they had them burned or buried with them, as the marvelous horse Felaróf was buried with Eorl the Young.

The royal hall of the Rohirrim, Meduseld (Old English for mead-hall), was a typical great hall in the Teutonic tradition. With its roof and doorposts of gold, it is reminiscent of Hrodgar's hall Heorot in *Beowulf*. Heorot's gables were covered with hammered gold and the light reflected from them could be seen far off. The completion of both Heorot and Meduseld was celebrated with feasting.[4] Because it was envisioned as the dwelling of a solar god as well as a royal hall, Odin's residence, Valhalla, was also described as a hall glittering with gold.

A typically Teutonic mythic position is filled by the Lady of the Rohirrim, Eowyn. As an armored princess on horse-

2 *Ibid.*, p. 235.
3 *Ibid.*, p. 93.
4 *Beowulf*, 76–85, 306–311.

back, Eowyn resembles the Valkyries who rode out to over-see the battlefield. Valkyries are most often depicted in pagan art as welcoming warriors to Valhalla with horns of mead, as Eowyn welcomed Aragorn to Meduseld. Sometimes Valkyries in myth were beautiful, sometimes they were fearsome.[5] This ambiguity of appearance is also seen in some accounts of the Grail Messenger in the Arthurian Cycle. The Grail Messenger sometimes appeared first as a hag, then when the quest of the Grail had been completed, appeared as a beautiful damsel. The same transformation took place in the women who represented the sovereignty of Ireland in Irish myths.[6] Eowyn underwent a similar transformation when her love for Faramir changed her from a chill, desperate warrior-woman to a gentle healer and bride.

An authentic depiction of Teutonic and Celtic practices is seen in the description of Théoden's burial and funeral feast. The building of the barrow, with the honored dead and his arms placed in a stone chamber, heaped over with earth and turf, is accurately described. The drinking of a goblet in memory of the deceased, as was done for Théoden, was called "drinking the *minne*." In Old High German, the word *minne*, signifying the drinking, also had the connotation of the draught, the memory, and the loved one. At the death of kings, this Teutonic ceremony was accompanied by the making of solemn vows.[7] At Théoden's funeral feast, Eowyn and Faramir were trothplighted, their vow directly following the drinking of the memory.

[5] Davidson, *Scandinavian Mythology*, p. 41.
[6] Loomis, *Celtic Myth and Arthurian Romance*, p. 299.
[7] *Grimm*, p. 59.

BARD

Bard the Bowman, who killed the dragon in *The Hobbit*, was an unusual hero. His qualities were not appreciated by his townsfellows and he was unrecognized as a hero until he had actually destroyed the dragon from the Lonely Mountain. After the refugees of the dragon-blasted Lake-town realized his achievement and his interest in their welfare, they chose him as new Lord of Dale. Bard's opportunity for heroism lay in three gifts: the gift of prophecy, an unfailing arrow, and the understanding of birds.

With his prophetic insight, Bard made gloomy predictions that made him unpopular. It was this gift, however, that caused him to anticipate the dragon's coming and warn the people of Lake-town.

The unfailing arrow with which Bard shot the dragon was an heirloom. It had been passed from father to son down a line descended from Girion, Lord of Dale, whose realm had been destroyed by the dragon when it entered the region one hundred and seventy-one years before.

From the point of view of myth, the most familiar part of Bard's story was his inherited understanding of birds. This allowed him to learn the dragon's weak point from an old thrush that had listened to Bilbo and the Dwarves.

In many myths and folk tales it was understood that birds and beasts spoke among themselves and were aware of events distant in time and place. In Tolkien's works, too, some animals spoke in their own languages, while others, such as the eagles, spoke the Common Speech.

In myth, the special knowledge that birds and beasts had was sometimes supernatural, that is, prophetic knowledge or knowledge of what people thought secretly, but was more often based on the nature of the birds and beasts themselves. Birds go farther afield and see more than men do from the ground, and animals can listen unnoticed to secret conversations. The old thrush that warned Bard was such an unregarded listener, but the prophetic power that readied Bard for combat with the dragon was Bard's own.

In folk tales, the special knowledge of animals was often disclosed to a hero who profited considerably by it. Many such heroes were, like Bard, undistinguished people until after they had acted upon the magically received information. In such stories the basic theme, no doubt that which appealed to Tolkien and which he incorporated in the story of Bard, is the implication that if a person has qualities which are unrecognized by his fellows, the wild beasts still know his true worth and have the power to aid him.

A typical folk tale of this type is a Basque story about an honest boy named Piarres who never learned anything except the speech of birds. He reported the birds' prophecies to his unbelieving father, who was so angered that he set his son adrift in the sea. Piarres was rescued, and the birds helped him to become a king's counselor, to fulfill their prophecies, and to win the hand of a princess.[1]

The appeal of Piarres' story lies in the resolution of universal problems between children and elders. It holds out hope to the many children who are called simpletons because they will not learn the things important to their parents, but spend their time in pursuits of interest only to themselves, comparable to Piarres' learning of bird-language. It also gives hope to children unjustly disbelieved, promising full compensation for undeserved punishment. In the course of Piarres' story,

[1] Carpenter, *Tales of a Basque Grandmother*, p. 83.

he was raised up and his father was humbled, the universal desire of youth. Only then could both father and son forgive one another.

A common way of gaining knowledge or inspiration in myth was to eat, usually by accident, magic food intended for someone else, usually an evil person who was fully aware of the food's potential. In some cases such food gave understanding of birds. One of the better-known magic-food stories is "The White Snake" from the Grimms' collection.[2] In this story, a king's servant ate a bit of baked white snake intended for the king. Immediately upon tasting it, he developed the gift of understanding birds and beasts. With this knowledge he aided some creatures which in turn helped him to pass the tests needed to win a proud princess.

"The White Snake" differs from most magic-food stories in that the king for whom the food was intended was not evil, but a good king and very wise, as a result of his habitual food. Furthermore, the servant did not eat the food accidentally, but made a deliberate attempt to find out the king's secret. The lesson of this universal type of story is that all good acts are recognized and rewarded. It is suggested that the system of rewarding good is so all-encompassing that even the birds and beasts take part in it, and repay good done even when it is unrecognized by humans.

A more typical story of magic food that gives understanding of birds occurs in the epic of Sigurd, who, like Bard, was an unrecognized hero who killed a dragon with an ancestral weapon. In the *Volsungsaga*, the smith Regin adopted Sigurd, reforged Sigurd's ancestral sword, and sent Sigurd to kill Regin's brother, Fafnir, who had become a dragon. When

[2] Jakob and Wilhelm Grimm, *German Folk Tales*, pp. 124–126.

the dragon was slain, Regin told Sigurd to roast the dragon's heart for him, planning first to derive supernatural powers from eating the heart and then to murder Sigurd. While roasting the heart, Sigurd burned his thumb on it and put his thumb in his mouth. He immediately obtained the gift of inspiration and the understanding of birds. Listening to two nuthatches on the branches above him, he learned of Regin's plot. With this knowledge he was able to kill Regin and escape.[3]

Sigurd was an unrecognized hero, Regin's puppet, when he killed the dragon. He did not become recognized as a hero until he rescued the Valkyrie Brynhild from her hill of fire and won her love.

In both Sigurd's and Bard's stories, supernatural intervention, the message of the birds, told the hero what he must do. In this way he was singled out and rewarded for otherwise unrecognized virtues. However, the heroic acts that they are remembered for consisted of taking the fleeting opportunity given them and doing the deeds that no one else could face.

Bard's purpose in *The Hobbit* was to be the dragon-slayer, to take on the part of Beowulf in the burglar-dragon-and-hero plot. Rather than choosing an established leader, such as the Master of Lake-town, for this venture, Tolkien produced a new character, an unrecognized hero, although of royal stock, who by his heroic acts established himself as a leader and was chosen as ruler by his people.

These attributes of Bard's prefigure those of Aragorn, the grim Ranger of royal blood who was greeted with suspicion by most peoples. Even Bard's three gifts are comparable to

[3] Snorri Sturluson, *The Prose Edda*, p. 111–115.

Aragorn's. The Ranger was credited with an understanding of birds and beasts, he made several important prophetic statements, and he bore a famed ancestral weapon. The pattern of Bard's heroism, itself based on myth, was expanded in the character of Aragorn, producing a more complex and more myth-oriented hero. In the transformation, the role of the hero's weapon was enhanced and the talent of understanding birds was largely ignored.

Bard's heroic act in slaying the dragon was also unparalleled by any single outstanding act on the part of Aragorn. This may be because *The Lord of the Rings* is more spiritual or ethical in its motivation and its victories are more subtle than those in *The Hobbit*, which is an adventure and thrives on fundamental, tangible acts and results.

BEORN

Beorn is the Old English word for man or hero, and is related to *bjorn*, the Danish, Swedish, and Icelandic word for bear. Beorn, in *The Hobbit*, was heroic in his size and strength, but more notable for his supernatural ability to take on the form of a huge bear. Such transformations are basic to myth.

The concept of men changing into animals is ancient and universal. There are numerous myths of gods and heroes who could assume animal forms. Sometimes this was a means of escape, as in the case of the shape-shifting Greek god Proteus. Sometimes two divinities changed shape in a contest, as did the Gobán Saor's daughter and a demon. Most often this was done, as in Beorn's case, in order to partake of the natural and supernatural qualities of the animal.

The transformation of a man into an animal was often effected by his assuming a garment made of the skin of the animal involved. As early as the Paleolithic Era, shamen seem to have disguised themselves as animals, according to the interpretation of certain cave paintings. Studies of shamen in historic times indicate that the transformation into animals attributed to them is an important source of their power.

Several interesting cases of shape-changing to gain the attributes of an animal occur in the *Volsungsaga*, an important influence on Tolkien's works. In one episode, Sigmund and Sinfjöth put on wolfskins, unaware that these were enchanted. The skins transformed them into wolves, and they remained in that form until the tenth day, when the spell was temporarily lifted. Taking this opportunity, the heroes burned the skins and broke the spell.[1] The story of Sigurd's adventures in the *Volsungsaga* began with the tragedy of Otter, a man who could take on the form of an otter and was killed in that form by the god Loki. Andvari, the Dwarf whose treasure was taken by Loki to compensate Otter's father for his son's death, often took the form of a pike living under a waterfall. Otter's brother Fafnir killed his father for the gold-hoard and transformed himself into a dragon to guard the treasure.[2]

It is significant that Tolkien chose the bear for Beorn's alternate form. Reverence for bears was common wherever they existed. As early as the Upper Paleolithic Era, the cave bear seems to have been revered. It was depicted in cave art and bear skulls have been found in cave niches and in a man-made cist.

Beliefs in the supernatural qualities of bears were common in Scandinavia. The Norse considered the bear a rational being and king of the animals. Bears were not only revered,

[1] Tonnelat, "Teutonic Mythology," *New Larousse Encyclopedia of Mythology*, p. 277.
[2] Davidson, *Scandinavian Mythology*, p. 100.

but it was believed that men could take on a bear's shape. A variety of traditions exist about humans in bear form. In Norway it was believed that Laplanders had the power to turn into bears. A Danish song tells how the transformation of a man into a bear was brought about by his wearing an iron collar. Unusually destructive bears were thought to be were-bears.[3]

Bodvar Biarki, an example of a bear-warrior comparable to Beorn, was a warrior of the Danish king Hrolf Kraki. He was supposed to have fought, as Beorn did in the Battle of Five Armies, in the likeness of a great bear against which the enemy was powerless. While his bear-spirit fought, the warrior himself remained at home, seemingly asleep.[4]

The best-known bear-warriors were the fierce Berserks, whose name apparently means "bear-shirt." They wore bear and wolf pelts and howled like beasts. They formed the bodyguard of the heathen kings of Norway and considered themselves to be warriors of Odin.[5]

Another feature of Beorn's story also belongs to mythic tradition. His gruesome treatment of the Orc, whose head he impaled, and of the wolf, whose skin he nailed up, was unexceptional. The Teutons commonly hung up the heads and skins of sacrificial animals and impaled the heads of enemies. A reflection of these practices may even be seen in the Grimms' folk tale "The Goosegirl,"[6] in which the hung-up head of the faithful horse Falada spoke to the cheated princess.

Tolkien's development of a sympathetic character from a were-bear is typical of his device of first presenting heroes

---

[3] Grimm, *Teutonic Mythology*, vol. III, p. 1097.
[4] Davidson, p. 40.
[5] *Ibid.*, p. 38.
[6] Jakob and Wilhelm Grimm, *German Folk Tales*, p. 323.

as grim and unprepossessing. The depiction of the bearlike man as solitary, irritable, unpredictable, and vengeful, but with a sense of warmth and humor, is an engaging one. The man and the bear had the same qualities: Beorn's personality did not change with his form. In the Battle of Five Armies, Beorn fought with the ferocity of his huge and powerful shape, but protected the fallen Dwarf, Thorin Oakenshield, with human tenderness.

THE WILD MEN

The Wild Men were for the most part the adversaries of the Men of the West. The wild Easterlings and Southrons provided much of Sauron's fighting force. Saruman made an army of the Dunlendings to fight the Rohirrim with whom they had an age-old rivalry over the land of Rohan. The Dead of the White Mountains were a forbidding force that guarded the subterranean Paths of the Dead. Most curious of the Wild Men were the Woses, unexpectedly faithful guides and aids against the Enemy, although they lived a savage, untaught existence hidden from other men.

THE WOSES AND THE DUNLENDINGS

The Woses and the Dunlendings were two wild peoples, related in some way, who played opposite parts in the history of their neighbors, the Rohirrim. The Woses had been thoughtlessly hunted by the Rohirrim, but during the War of the Ring they unexpectedly aided the Riders. The Dunlendings, however, had been violent rivals of the Rohirrim from the time the Horselords settled Rohan, which had once been a part of Dunland.

The Woses are derived from Teutonic mythology. Their name appears in Old English as *Wuduwasa* and in Middle English in the forms Woodwose and Wodwos. These words were applied to a sort of satyrlike sylvan creature. The Woodwose was supposed to be small, wild, leafy, hairy, and belonged to the same tradition as the waltman, woodsmen, and wildfolk of Teutonic myth.[1] The Woodwose became a symbol in heraldry, and the name is retained in the surname Woodhouse, evolved from the spelling Woodouse.

The various Teutonic woods-creatures related to the Woodwose also inspired Tolkien's Ents. Tolkien adapted one idea (treelike, semihuman, supernatural beings) to two entirely different ends. He characterized the Ents as tall, personified trees, while he depicted the Woses as small, forest-dwelling humans.

The Woses in *The Lord of the Rings* retained few mythic attributes other than their name, physical characteristics, and antiquity. They were described as small, stumpy, and gnarled, with mosslike beards. Tolkien gave them the character of noble savages: honorable, wood-wise, and inscrutable, and speaking a predictable, stock pidgin.

The Dunlendings were not given as much attention. However, they were known to have had a long history in the areas north and west of the White Mountains and to have always been warriors. They were related to the People of the Mountains (who became the Dead of the Paths of the Dead) in the south, and to the men of Bree in the north.

The Dunlendings (meaning "Dunlanders") were named

[1] Grimm, *Teutonic Mythology*, vol. IV, p. 1462.

for their dark coloring. *Dunn* is an Old English word for brown or a dark color, from which the modern word *dun* (a dull brown) is derived. However, the name is also another of Tolkien's Old English puns because the standard Old English compound word *dún-land* means down-land or hilly land, as contrasted with *feld-land*, plain or level land. This meaning of *dun* is retained in the modern words *downs* and *dune*.

At the time of the War of the Ring, the Dunlendings lived in Dunland, west of the White Mountains and of the southern end of the Misty Mountains. However, at one time they inhabited not only that region, but western Rohan and the vales of the White Mountains as well.

The exact relationship between the Woses and the Dunlendings is uncertain. The evidences of relationship lie in some mysterious sculptures and two curious words. The words are *Dru* and *Púkel*. Púkel is another adaptation from the Old English. Spelled *púcel* or *puckle*, the word meant a goblin or demon, and was a synonym for Woodwose. The word is related to the Irish *púca* or *pooka*, a sprite, and to Shakespeare's Puck. The Druadan Forest, where the Woses lived, must have been named for them (*adan* means "man" in Sindarin). Thus the Woses must have been known since the arrival of the Sindarin-speaking men of Gondor as Druedain (*edain* is Sindarin for "men"). The word Dru appears again on one of Pauline Baynes' maps of Middle-earth; the part of Dunland south of the Isen River is there called Druwaith Iuar. This title is glossed as "Old Púkel-land." This recalls the Púkel-men, sculptures resembling Woses, carved by forgotten people on the cliff road to Dunharrow. These may indicate that the Woses and the Dunlendings had a common ancestor, that their lands once overlapped, or that they once inhabited adjacent lands.

The builders of Dunharrow and the sculptors of the Púkel-men were unknown. They may have been the Dunlendings or their kin who became the Dead and whose ghosts lingered in the area. Tolkien states that the purpose of Dunharrow was forgotten, and suggests that it was either an ancient city, a secret temple, or a royal burial ground. However, a guess may be made. The word harrow is derived from the Old English *hearg* by the same evolution that forms *barrow* from *beorg*. *Hearg* was the word for a sacred place, a temple.[2]

THE DEAD

In *The Lord of the Rings* there are two accounts of dead peoples whose spirits still frequented their place of death. These are the dead Men, Elves, and Orcs of the Dead Marshes and the Dead of the White Mountains, down whose paths Aragorn led the Dúnedain.

The Dead of the Marshes were the combatants in the last alliance of Men and Elves against the forces of Sauron at the end of the Second Age. Although an age of the world had passed since they had died, the images of their faces, beautiful or monstrous, were still seen by Frodo, Sam, and Sméagol. These faces, submerged beneath the slimy surface, were not those of actual corpses, but were an illusion created by the Enemy. The vision of faces was accompanied by "candles of corpses," luminous veils and shreds of light that hovered over the water and led astray the few travelers that entered the Marshes.

It is a common myth that spirits produce deceiving lights.

[2] *Ibid.*, vol. I, p. 68.

It was a popular belief in Germany, still current when Grimm wrote in 1883, that souls that had not attained heavenly peace flew about as birds in firy shape.[1]

The weird lights formed by marsh gas or natural electricity have many names in myth. The most common are *ignis fatuus* (literally "foolish fire," that is, deluding light), Saint Elmo's fire, and Will-o'-the-Wisp, so called because it resembles a burning wisp of straw. Many of the names refer to quick movement and deception, as does Tolkien's term, "tricksey lights." Tolkien's reference to this phenomenon suggests that the spirits of the men and Elves were under Sauron's enchantment, unable to rest until his destruction.

The Dead in the White Mountains were doomed to walk the earth for oath-breaking. When Isildur first came to Middle-earth, he set up a huge black sphere of stone at Erech where the King of the White Mountains swore allegiance to him. However, when the people of the mountains were called to fight with him against Sauron, they would not come. They had worshiped Sauron secretly and would not oppose him. Isildur cursed them, vowing that they would never rest until they were called by his heir and fulfilled their oath. They remained a hidden people for a little while, but soon perished. Their spirits haunted the White Mountains and were seen oftenest at the Stone of Erech and at the entrance to the Paths of the Dead in Dunharrow. They gathered at these places in times of trouble, awaiting the heir of Isildur.

Acting upon the prophecy of Malbeth made over two thousand years before, Aragorn took the Paths of the Dead, led the Dúnedain to Erech, and called the Dead to fulfill their oath. He led them to Pelargir where they dispersed Sauron's

---

[1] Grimm, *Teutonic Mythology*, vol. II, p. 916.

allies, the Corsairs of Umbar, and were released from Isildur's curse.

These Dead recall the Teutonic myths of the Furious Host, unquiet dead who were doomed to walk, ride, or hunt in a company for eternity. Just as the gathering of the Dead preceded times of trouble, the marching of the Furious Host as an army portended war.[2]

In the context of the legends of the Furious Host, it was significant that Aragorn had the power to keep the Dead behind him in their impetuous ride to Pelargir. Norwegian tradition has it that living men have been caught up in the Host and dragged along with them in their furious haste.[3]

Unlike the usually thunderous Host, Tolkien's Dead were preternaturally silent. The silence of the dead is also traditional. Even the dead returned to life were often mute. In the Welsh story "Branwen the Daughter of Llyr," in *The Mabinogion*, Bendigeid Vran gave Matholwych King of Ireland a cauldron such that if a slain man were put in it, he would be as well as ever the next day, except that he would never regain the power of speech.[4] In the Finnish *Kalevala*, the slain hero Lemminkainen could not speak even after his mother fitted the shreds of his dismembered body together and restored him to life. He only regained the power of speech after treatment with a divine salve.[5]

---

[2] *Ibid.*, p. 937.
[3] *Ibid.*, p. 946.
[4] *The Mabinogion*, p. 37.
[5] Guirand, "Finno-Ugric Mythology," *New Larousse Encyclopedia of Mythology*, p. 302.

12

The Old Gods

A NUMBER of the beings in Tolkien's works are completely supernatural. These include the Valar, Wizards, Elves, Dwarves, Bombadil and Goldberry, Ents, and such evil creatures as Sauron, the Orcs, and the Balrog. They belong to classes of beings which, at one time or another and in one form or another, were worshiped as gods by Celts, Teutons, and indeed most European peoples. Beings analogous to them were revered in most parts of the world.

It may seem incongruous that beings such as Ents or Elves could command worship, but the creatures that we read about in folk tales have been diminished in dignity and power since the introduction of Christianity. Some of the beings were never gods in the sense that we understand the word today, but were protective spirits and embodied essences of the land. Others, including the Celtic Tuatha Dé Danann, were among the most powerful and most venerated of the gods, which, under Christianity, became thought of only as a fairy folk, retaining few of their powers.

The supernatural beings in *The Lord of the Rings* form a hierarchy based on their relative levels of power. Like the hierarchies common to most pantheons, Tolkien's is not clearly defined. Specific contests between the different types of

beings were infrequent, and the outcomes were often inde-
cisive. The beings' relative powers sometimes also changed
with the time and place. For example, Sauron, after his defeat
at the end of the Second Age, spent a thousand years gathering
strength before he again became a power to be reckoned with.
During the War of the Ring, the Ringwraiths increased in
power as they drew closer to their master in Mordor. The
One Ring, too, gathered force as it approached its forging
place. The process was reversed for the Phial of Galadriel,
which became useless in the center of Sauron's realm.

An overview of Tolkien's supernatural beings and their relationships to one another and to the old gods is given briefly
here in the order in which the beings are discussed in the
subsequent sections.

The supreme being of Tolkien's pantheon is the One, probably called Eru (Elves and men are referred to as *Erusen*,
"the children of God"). Obedient to the One are lesser gods,
the Valar, sometimes referred to as angelic powers. The Valar
were the demiurgic creators of the world, its guardians and its
fates. They were worshiped and invoked by both the mortals
and immortals of Middle-earth, whose destinies the Valar determined.

The wizards are comparable to various European gods, including the Scandinavian Odin and the Celtic Merlin. There
are levels of power among the wizards themselves, but Gandalf
clearly became the wisest and greatest, and may always have
been so. He derived great power from the Elven Ring which
he wore secretly. With this ring he was able to vanquish the
Balrog, almost his equal, and to repel the Nazgûl, who also
derived their power from rings. Even Sauron seemed evenly
matched by Gandalf's will when they contested at a distance
over Frodo, who was wearing the One Ring on Amon Hen.

The Elves of Middle-earth were invested with some of the original majesty and reverence of Elves in myth. Tolkien's Elves are immortal and can wield unearthly power. This power was such that the approach of Gildor's Elves in the Shire was enough to turn aside a Black Rider. Glorfindel, a powerful Elf-lord, drove off Ringwraiths unassisted when the wraiths lay in ambush at the Bridge of Mitheithel. Glorfindel had done so before: one thousand years earlier he had driven off the Witch-king who threatened Eärnur, Captain of Gondor. The greatest of the Elves in power and wisdom were Elrond and Galadriel. They derived much of their power from Elven Rings with which they established secret lands where evil things could not come.

Dwarves were probably never worshiped in European mythology, and may even have represented spirits of the dead. Although long-lived, they were mortal, but they lived apart from men. Their power, both in myth and in Tolkien's works, appears in their association with the semimagical arts of smithcraft and metallurgy, and their ability to make magical things. In Scandinavian myth, the Dwarves furnished the great gods with their essential symbols and weapons. The Dwarves of Middle-earth were known for their considerable strength and endurance.

Bombadil and Goldberry have the characteristics of deities of woods and water. They are humbler than the High Elves, but have powers as lasting and potent as the earth itself. They are guardians, not unlike the Valar, but their realm is one small secret land where they are all but forgotten by the rest of the world. Bombadil's power was in his complete independence: even the Ring had no hold over him. However, even in his land he was not all-powerful. Glorfindel predicted that if Sauron overcame the West, Bombadil too would fall, "Last as he was First."

The Ents and Trolls are like the European spirits of trees and stones respectively. The Giants in myth, on whom they were based, were not differentiated, but were now treelike, now stonelike, now wise, now dull, now good, now evil. Tolkien separated giant-kind, giving to Ents the dignity of trees and their power to cleave rock, and to Trolls the mindless, ponderous strength of animated stone.

The evil creatures in Tolkien's works also have their counterparts in mythology. Sauron can be compared to a number of dark and baleful gods: Pluto, Balar, and, primarily, Odin. Since Sauron was never encountered at close range, it is difficult to guess the full extent of his power. However, he seems, like the orthodox Satan, to have been incapable of material creation, but to have produced illusions and to have corrupted what came within his long reach. The Orcs ultimately take their name from a god of the underworld, the Latin Orcus, and are reflections of all the demons that plague mankind in mythology. The Balrog of Moria resembles Surt, the adversary of the Scandinavian gods. Surt wielded the fire that destroyed the world in the accounts of Ragnarök, the Fatal Destiny of the Gods.

Tolkien knew the potentialities of the creatures he portrayed, and returned to them some of the awe that was given them before they became the bogies and pixies of bedtime stories. He gave them motivations that can be understood by humans, yet they cannot be mistaken for human beings, and, for good or evil, they maintain a pervasive pagan power.

THE VALAR

The Valar (singular: Vala) were angelic powers or divinities. They were the demiurgic creators of the world and were the world's guardians.[1] They determined the destiny of Middle-earth, as described in the section on Fate. The Valar were under the direction of a supreme being, the One, who guided them in the creation of the world. (The only mention of this supreme being is made in Appendix A of *The Return of the King* when the Blessed Realm was attacked by the Nú-menoreans and the Valar called upon the One to protect it.)[2]

The word Vala is Old Norse. It means "seeress" and may be related to the word *valkyrie*.[3] Vala was used as the name of several Scandinavian seeresses; the "Völuspâ," the first poem of the *Elder Edda*, was named after such a Vala. This Eddic seeress omnisciently described the creation of the world and its fated destruction and rebirth.[4] In view of these connotations, Tolkien chose an appropriate name for the omniscient and fate-determining Valar.

The Valar are also comparable to the Norns of Scandinavian mythology. The Norns were three supernatural wisewomen who lived under the world-tree Yggdrasil and spun and wove the fates of mortals. They were called *Wyrds*, meaning "Fates"; from them were derived the prophetic three weird sisters in *Macbeth*.

As dispensers of fate, Norns, Seeresses, and Fates visited the homes of newborn babies and prophesied their futures. "Briar-rose" or "Sleeping Beauty" is a familiar story with this theme.[5] In a similar way, the Valar watched over and guarded the people of Middle-earth and to some degree determined the fate of individuals.

---

[1] Tolkien and Swann, *The Road Goes Ever On*, p. 66.
[2] Tolkien, *The Return of the King*, p. 317.
[3] Grimm, *Teutonic Mythology*, vol. I, p. 98.
[4] *Ibid.*, p. 403.
[5] *Ibid.*, p. 410.

The most revered of the Valar was Varda, their queen. She was envisioned as standing radiant and queenly on Mount Everwhite, watching over Middle-earth and listening to the hymns sung to her and the prayers of those in need.

The name Varda means "Exalted" in Quenya. In Sindarin, Varda was called Elbereth ("Star-queen"). She was also referred to as Tintalle in Quenya and Gilthoniel in Sindarin, both meaning "Star-kindler." Her Sindarin title Fanuilos means "Everwhite Divine Figure," a title derived from the majestic, radiant figures (*fana*, meaning "veils" or "figures") assumed by the Valar when seen by mortals. These figures had the appearance of those of Elves or Men, but were tall, regal, and filled with light.

As the primary feminine deity of Middle-earth, Varda partook of the qualities of a number of goddesses. Her title, "Exalted," is the same as that of Brighid, the principal goddess of the Celts.[6] As Star-kindler and Queen of the angelic Valar, Varda is comparable to the Greek goddess Eos, Mother of the Stars, and the Virgin Mary, Queen of the Angels.

Varda is in the tradition of great goddesses, such as Demeter, who were probably derived from the mythology of ancient matriarchal cultures. As it was the goddesses and not their lords who were important in these myths, so it was with Varda. It was to her that the Elves sang and to whom they appealed in need, while very little mention at all was made of Manwe, the Elder King, the Lord of the Valar.

As a beautiful divinity who answered the calls of the distressed and dispensed immortality, Varda is reminiscent of the Teutonic Valkyries. The Valkyries, often beautiful, were heaven-dwelling women who answered the calls of heroes

[6] MacCana, *Celtic Mythology*, p. 35.

and finally conducted them to immortality in Valhalla. Some seem to have wakened fallen warriors to life again,[7] as Gandalf was returned to life, apparently by the Valar, on the peak of Silvertine.

The dwellings of Varda and Manwe on Mount Everwhite, the highest mountain in the world, are like the mountain homes and thrones of gods throughout the world. The most familiar example is Mount Olympus, the dwelling of the Greek gods. Odin, too, had a high seat, Hlidskialf, from which he could see and hear all that happened on earth. Such mountain homes establish the gods as exalted beings and as viewers of all that occurs below. Mountain dwellings form a link between heaven, where the gods were thought to live, and earth, where they ruled.

Most of the Valar were envisioned as remote, physically and spiritually, from the human world. This was not the case with Oromë, the Huntsman of the Valar. He visited Middle-earth where he was known as Araw by the Sindarin Elves and as Béma by mortals. He brought two significant gifts from the West to mankind — the wild white cattle called the Kine of Araw and the ancestors of the horses of Rohan called the *mearas*.

The wild kine are principally remembered because they provided an important heirloom of the house of the Ruling Stewards of Gondor. Vorondil the Hunter, Steward to King Eärnil, brought a horn of one of the kine back from a hunting expedition to Rhûn. This horn was bound in silver and was given to Vorondil's son Mardil Voronwe, the first Ruling Steward. It was passed down twenty-five generations of Stewards until it was broken when the last Ruling Steward's son, Boromir, was slain.

[7] Grimm, p. 442.

The *mearas* ("horses" in Old English) were beautiful, swift, often white or silver-grey, and almost untamable. The introduction of their ancestors to Middle-earth was attributed to Béma by the Rohirrim. Eorl, who became the first king of Rohan, chose one of these horses, Felaróf, as his royal steed. Felaróf ("very valiant, strong" in Old English) became the ancestor of the line of the horses of the kings. They would only bear the kings of Rohan or their sons until Shadowfax permitted Gandalf to tame him.

The creatures that Oromë brought to mankind were animals that have long been revered by man. Greeks, Romans, Celts, and Teutons honored white cattle and deemed them particularly worthy for sacrifice. The *Elder Edda* credits a cow, Adumbla, with having taken part in the creation. The horse, which was also sacrificed, was considered sacred to Frey by the Scandinavians and to Epona by the Celts.

Probably owing to his gift of royal horses, the Rohirrim revered the Huntsman of the Valar, giving him the name Béma, meaning "Trumpet" in Old English. The only image that the reader is given of any Vala comes from a comparison of Oromë to a king of Rohan. When Théoden led the Rohirrim into battle on the Pelennor Field, he was said to be like "Oromë the Great in the battle of the Valar when the world was young."[8] The relationship between the Rohirrim and Oromë is the only indication that mortals other than the Dúnedain venerated the Valar or any other gods.

The Vala most influential in the history of Middle-earth was Morgoth, the Great Enemy and Sauron's master. He became a traitor to the Blessed Realm and left it for a life of exile in Middle-earth. His sin, one of the recurring sins in Tolkien's works (also Thorin's sin in *The Hobbit*) was covet-

[8] Tolkien, p. 113.

ousness. He desired, and stole, the Silmarilli, three crystal jewels that held the light of the Two Trees of Valinor. When Morgoth left the land of the Valar, he poisoned the Two Trees of Light so that, as possessor of the jewels, he alone could view their radiance. Morgoth's action, which brought about the first alliance of Elves and Men, was the starting point of the history of Middle-earth and can be compared with myths of creation. Morgoth's pride, covetousness, and exile are reminiscent of those of the fallen angel Lucifer.

The Two Trees of Valinor recall the Tree of Life and the Tree of the Knowledge of Good and Evil in Genesis. Like the Two Trees, the trees of the Garden of Eden had supernatural powers and grew in a divine land now beyond mortal reach. The theme of pairs of trees in creation myths is also found in the *Elder Edda* where the gods found two trees on the shore of the newly created world and transformed them into the first man and woman, named Ask and Embla, Ash and Elm.[9]

In the Valar and the One who ruled them, Tolkien established a pervasive but unobtrusive theology for Middle-earth. These gods were alive and responsive to their worshipers, taking an active part in their fate. The worshipers lived securely in their belief, which, though it colored all their actions, was seldom spoken of. Such imaginary pantheons are not uncommon in the writings of Christian authors, but they are seldom so subtly and sympathetically portrayed.

THE WIZARDS

At the end of the first thousand years of the Third Age, when the power of the enemy was growing in Mirkwood, the Valar

[9] Grimm, vol. II, p. 560.

sent the Order of the Istari, or Wizards, out of the West to unite the free peoples against Sauron. There were five members in the Order, only three of whom are mentioned in Tolkien's works. Among men they were called Radagast, Saruman, and Gandalf. They appeared as old men and each wore his specific color. They had differing powers and talents, but were not permitted to use their power directly to contest the Enemy.

Least was said about Radagast. His name is that of a Slavonic god, Radegast or Radihost, who was associated with the Roman god Mercury. This is appropriate: Mercury in turn was identified with the Greek god Hermes, the god of alchemists. Alchemists were considered wizards, and it was for a wizard that Tolkien appropriated this name. Radegast's pervasive influence in Eastern Europe where he was worshiped is exemplified by the important role played by a priest of Radegast in *Mlada*, an opera by Rimsky-Korsakov, based on Slavonic mythology.

The name Radegast is derived from *rad* ("glad") and *radost* ("joy") because Radegast was a god of bliss, whom Grimm associated with Odin as a personification of Wish.[1] The Slavonic Radegast was also described as a sure counselor and a god of strength and honor.[2] Both of Tolkien's good wizards were indeed important counselors, and the wizard Radagast's honor was also significant: even Saruman would not try to corrupt him.

The powers attributed to Radagast the Brown, those of changing shape and color and of speaking with birds and beasts, are universal in myth. These powers identify this

[1] Grimm, *Teutonic Mythology*, vol. III, p. xxx.
[2] Alexinski, "Slavonic Mythology," *"New Larousse Encyclopedia of Mythology*, p. 294.

obscure wizard with the earliest form of wizard, the shaman.

Where Radagast resembled the shaman, Saruman was like
the alchemist, preferring secret devices, mechanisms, and shows
of power. Curunír, Saruman's name in Sindarin, meant "Man
of Skill." The Old English name, *Searu-man*, is more telling;
it means "man of craft, devices, and wiles" and could have
either a good or bad connotation.
    Besides the secret engines of his alchemy, Saruman had all
the adjuncts of a medieval sorcerer: a tower from which to
view the stars, a magic staff, and the prophetic globe of the
crystal-gazer. His search for the skills to make or take a Ring
of Power is comparable in ambition and futility to the alchemists' search for the Philosophers' Stone.
    As leader of the wizards' White Council, Saruman was him-
self called the White. When he rejected the council, he re-
voked the title, scorned the purity of white, and adopted a
cloak of mingled colors as suggestive of vanity as the robe of
Joseph.

The most important of the wizards was Gandalf. He was
the prime mover of most of the West's efforts in the War of
the Ring. His leadership was based upon the power of prophecy, the supernatural force of his Elven Ring, and his superior
wisdom and common sense. However, for most of his life he
wandered Middle-earth as an unassuming, grey-cloaked pilgrim, his powers and purposes known only to a few.
    Gandalf's names refer to his appearance and to his super-
natural powers. The name Gandalf comes from the *Prose
Edda* where it was among the names of mythical Dwarves
which Tolkien adapted to name the Dwarves in *The Hobbit*.

The original form of this name was Ganndálf, which Young translates as "Sorcerer-elf."[3] Gandalf's Sindarin name, Mithrandir, meant "Grey Pilgrim." His Dwarvish name, Tharkûn, is reminiscent of the Orkish *sharkû* ("old man") from which Saruman's nickname "Sharkey" was derived. Gandalf's name in the south, Incánus, is Latin for "quite grey." Olórin, his name in the West, may come from the Old High German Alarûn and the Old Norse Ölrun, which meant "a prophetic or diabolic spirit" and later became the word for a mandrake root.

Gandalf's individual power was that of firemaker, which he exhibited in both *The Hobbit* and *The Lord of the Rings*. The source of this power was Narya, the Ring of Fire, one of the three Elven Rings. As firemaker, Gandalf was part of a significant mythic tradition. Fire was credited with purifying power and was associated with the sun and the seasonal cycle. The process of kindling ritual fires was a sacred tradition and only certain persons and tools could be involved. Thus Gandalf combined the most ancient art of the shaman, that of building fire needed for life, with the most advanced researches of the alchemist, those of using fire for explosive destruction.

Gandalf is one of the most complex characters in Tolkien's works, but he has a parallel in Malory's Merlin. These two wizards were both powerful, prophetic, inscrutable, and, suddenly, unexpectedly human. Each had the responsibility for the fortunes of a nation and its future king; each had a dramatic sense of suspense and a childlike love of concocting surprises.

Gandalf and Merlin both had obscure beginnings and mysterious endings to their lives. Gandalf came out of the West in the form of an aged man and returned to the West in the

[3] Snorri Sturluson, *The Prose Edda,* p. 41.

same form for eternal life. Merlin was divinely fathered in some accounts, and had probably himself been a Celtic god at one time. However, for the sake of the Church, he was popularly said to be the son of a demon.[4] Merlin, like Gandalf, was supposed to have become immortal, hidden, in a trance, in a mist or a cave or a tomb in which he was immured by the variously named enchantress, Nimue. In Welsh legend he was said to dwell in a glass castle on a western island (identified with Bardsley Island), as Gandalf lived eternally on the western islands of the Blessed Realm.

Merlin's early, sudden disappearance from *Le Morte Darthur* (out of the twenty-one books, Merlin appears only in the first four) is reflected in Gandalf's fall in Moria. Merlin was missed from the story, as Tolkien realized Gandalf would have been. Thereafter, Merlin's function as a prophet had to be taken over by a number of mysterious old men who seem little different from Merlin himself.

Gandalf was Aragorn's counselor in much the same way that Merlin was King Arthur's. For example, before the battle with eleven kings, King Arthur asked his barons to take the advice of Merlin in organizing their strategy. Comparably, in the Last Debate, Aragorn counseled the Captains of the West to rely on Gandalf's experience in their war with the Enemy. Gandalf's relationship to the whole company of the Ring is stated well by Loomis' description of Merlin. He was "an omniscient and omnipotent arranger of tests and master of ceremonies, with all good will conducting the heroes through the trials and struggles that will fall their lot."[5]

Although in character Gandalf is most like Merlin, his appearance is comparable to that of the Scandinavian god, Odin.

---

[4] Loomis, *Celtic Myth and Arthurian Romance*, p. 127.
[5] *Ibid.*, p. 136.

Odin, like Gandalf, was accomplished in magic, runes, and incantations, but he had a grisly, treacherous side to his character which Gandalf never possessed. However, like Gandalf, Odin was depicted as elderly, with a long grey beard. He was known as the Old God, indicating the antiquity of his worship as well as his elderly appearance. Among Odin's many names were Sidskegg ("Long-bearded One") and Harbard ("Grey-bearded One").[6] Odin was described as wearing a broad-brimmed hat, as was Gandalf, and a blue cloak typifying the sky of which he was lord, as Gandalf wore a blue cloak on his return from Gondor.

Odin's horse, Sleipnir ("Slippery"), a tall, white, magical steed, is one of the many magical horses that Gandalf's horse Shadowfax resembled. Tolkien took Shadowfax's name from a Scandinavian tradition in naming mythic horses, such as Hrimfaxi ("Rimymane") and Skinfaxi ("Shinymane"), the Horses of Night and Day.[7] The familiarity that existed between the wizard and his horse is similar to that between many heroes and their steeds: such horses in myth could often talk to their owners, or, like Shadowfax, understand human speech.

Another significant example of mythic horses in Gandalf's story is the illusion of white horses and riders that Gandalf sent down the Loudwater of Rivendell as it swept away the Black Riders. This illusion symbolized the power inherent in the Loudwater to repel evil from Rivendell. Such white horses of the water are a traditional matter of myth, where they often were sacred to the sun and the sea. In British myth, the waves were called the horses of the sun god Beli, because once the sun had seemingly sunk into the sea, they carried it through

[6] Snorri Sturluson, p. 49.
[7] Grimm, vol. I, p. 328.

the night to the east.[8] The Scottish kelpie, a supernatural water-beast that haunted the shore, often took the form of a horse. In poetry it is traditional to compare waves to horses, as Dylan Thomas did in his "Reminiscences of Childhood," when he saw the sea "roll in and out like that, white-horsed and full of fishes."[9]

The story of Gandalf as a whole, his mysterious advent and departure, and his purpose in Middle-earth, have significant parallels in the mythic Scandinavian kings from the sea. These kings came to land, often as foundling children, on ships from obscure origins. They became significantly concerned with the welfare of the country to which they came, and their reigns were crowned with prosperity. Then, as mysteriously as they had come, they returned by ship to unknown destinations.[10]

The best known example of such a king is Scyld, a king of Denmark described in *Beowulf*. He came as a foundling in a treasure ship and was sent away at his death in a richly laden funeral ship after a peaceful and prosperous reign.[11]

Gandalf's arrival by sea from the West, and his voyage back to the Blessed Realm after over two thousand years in Middle-earth, are comparable to the journeys of the kings from the sea. His influence for the welfare of Middle-earth was the greatest of anyone in his time, and although he was never himself a king, it was through his efforts that the kingdom was restored and Middle-earth attained peace.

[8] Graves, *The White Goddess*, p. 59.
[9] Thomas, "Reminiscences of Childhood," *Quite Early One Morning*, p. 3.
[10] Davidson, *Scandinavian Mythology*, p. 79.
[11] *Beowulf*, 4–52.

THE ELVES

Tolkien's Elves were tall and more beautiful than mortals. They had dark hair and grey eyes, except for those such as Galadriel and Glorfindel who belonged to the golden house of Finrod and had golden hair. The great among the Elves had supernatural powers and were foresighted. They held themselves aloof from men, and, when asked for counsel, gave only ambiguous answers in the tradition of oracles.

Elves in Celtic and Teutonic mythologies included not only the good and beautiful, but also the evil and grotesque. Some of the Elves were helpful only when treated in a particular way. Household and farmyard Elves would do chores if they were left simple foods, but if they were given clothing, they would consider themselves paid off and never return. Some were malicious, tangling a spinner's thread or leading travelers astray in the dark. Even the Sidhe, the Fair Folk of the Celts, could be merciless.

In general, Tolkien's Elves most resemble the Irish Sidhe and the Light Elves of the Eddas. The Sidhe were the remnants of the Tuatha Dé Danann, the old gods of Ireland, diminished, but retaining unearthly powers. They were tall, sometimes taller than mortals, and beautiful with more than human beauty. They were generally immortal, although some could die, as did some of the Elves in Tolkien's works. Also like the Eldar, the Sidhe controlled magic and were foresighted. The Sidhe did not intrude upon the world of men, nor did men invoke them.

The Teutonic Light Elves also formed a community separate from that of men. They had supernatural powers and great beauty. They were considered more divine than men

and had the gifts of prophecy and divination. They were well-
formed and symmetrical, unlike the misshapen Dwarves or
Dark Elves. The Elves were weavers while Dwarves were
smiths and miners. Elves were so long-lived that, when tricked
into disclosing their ages, they turned out to be as old as the
oldest forests and mountains. Like the Eldar, they loved music,
singing, and dancing.[1]

In Tolkien's works and in mythology, the words Elf, Eldar,
and Elder have a complex relationship. Elf is the word for a
member of a specific supernatural people. Eldar is the word
for Elves in Quenya, the classical Elvish language. (Eldar is
related to the Elvish word *el*, meaning "star.") The Elder
King was the Lord of the Valar. The Elder Days were the
days of the First Age when the Elves had dominion over the
world.

The word Eldar may have been suggested by the Old English word for Elves, *Yldra*, and the Scandinavian *huldre-folk*,
from *hyld*, the elder tree.[2] The elder tree is associated with
death, fairies, and witches. It blossoms in midsummer when
Elven-folk traditionally have power, its flowers are Elven-
white, and of all the trees in the forest it is the first to leaf out.[3]

In the Teutonic languages, Elf, Alf, Alp, and Albs are words
for Elves, related to the Latin *albus* ("white"). These names
are suggested by the pale garments and radiant beauty of this
people. Whiteness and brightness are consistently ascribed to
Teutonic Elves.

Tolkien's conception of Elvenhome is as ambiguous as is that
of the Celts. He seems to have had in mind two images of
Elvenhome and of the Queen of the Elves. One was an im-

[1] Grimm, *Teutonic Mythology*, vol. II, pp. 439–471.
[2] Grimm, vol. IV, p. 1416.
[3] Graves, *The White Goddess*, p. 185.

mortal island beyond the world, ruled by an angelic goddess
from a mountaintop. The other was a beautiful place within
the world, ruled by an immortal woman who was magical and
perilous, but not divine. These two visions are blended in
Tolkien's *Smith of Wootton Major*. They are also combined
in the sequence in which Galadriel projects a vision of herself
as she would have been as the ruler of the One Ring. At that
moment she seemed to be both herself and the angelic Varda.

These ambiguities are like those of Celtic Myth, where there
was no clear distinction between Elysium and Elvenhome and
various accounts were given of both. The world of the Sidhe
was sometimes comparable to the Blessed Realm. The Sidhe
were said to live, among other places, in Tír nan Og, the Land
of Youth, an island toward the setting sun. This otherworld's
queen was, like Varda, generally considered more important
than its king. However, it was sometimes supposed to have
as its lord Manannán Mac Lir (Son of the Sea) for whom the
Isle of Man was named. The name Manannán may have suggested the name of Manwe, the Elder King of the Blessed
Realm.

The Sidhe not only lived on western islands, but inside
barrows, under the earth, beneath the sea, or in secret places
on the earth, like Tolkien's Lórien. As in Lórien, where the
Company of the Ring lost all account of time, time was suspended in the Celtic otherworld. Sometimes heroes who penetrated the otherworld stayed only a day, but returned to find
the world changed by the passage of many years, and, once
they set foot to the earth, they became old themselves or
withered into dust. At other times, as in the Irish "Adventure
of Nera," which takes place at Samhain, the opposite is the
case. Nera spent a year in the otherworld and took a wife
from among the Sidhe, but when he returned, he found his

mortal companions still at the feast where he had left them. The purpose of this ambiguity, in myth as in *The Lord of the Rings*, is to enhance the alien, supernatural quality of the otherworld by suspending time, the one certainty in the mortal world.

Two of the most important descendants of Elves in the history of Middle-earth were Elrond Halfelven, the greatest of the Wise, and his brother Elros ("Star-foam"). Their lineage was of Elves and men mingled, both their parents having been half-Elven. At the end of the First Age, the Valar gave Elrond and Elros the choice of becoming either mortal or immortal. Elros chose mortality, assumed the title Tar-Minyatur, and became the first king of the Dúnedain on Númenor. Elrond chose immortality, lived for long ages of the world, and journeyed at last to the Undying Lands.

The story of Elrond and Elros follows the mythological theme of twin brothers. The birth of twins, an uncommon event, was often considered either an evil omen or a divine manifestation. Sometimes twins were thought to be the children of two fathers, one mortal and the other a god. This was the case of Castor and Pollux in Greek mythology. They were considered the sons of Leda, one by her mortal husband Tyndareus and the other by Zeus in the form of a swan. When Castor died in battle, Pollux mourned the fact that as an immortal he could not follow his brother to the underworld. Zeus, taking pity on him, transformed the brothers into the constellation Gemini, the Twins. In the case of Elrond and Elros, it was their father, Eärendil, who underwent celestial transformation, carrying the Silmaril as the morning star.

Eärendil was given considerable significance in the tales of the Elder Days because his story formed the culmination of the story of the Silmarilli. In Tolkien's works, Eärendil was a mariner who sailed the coasts of Middle-earth and traveled far west into Evernight. He returned to Middle-earth and wedded half-Elven Elwing who crowned him with the Silmaril. His ship was then blown by a supernatural wind to Elvenhome and the land of the Valar. There he was appointed to sail the sky as an immortal, bearing the brilliant Silmaril as a celestial symbol of hope to the peoples of Middle-earth.

In Teutonic mythology, stories about Earendil are of great antiquity. According to Scandinavian mythology, Earendil (called by various names including Earendel, Orentil, and Erentel) was the first hero, son of King Eigel. He was a mariner who suffered shipwreck and sheltered with the master fisherman, Eisen. He won Breide ("Bright"), fairest of women. She corresponds well with Elwing, the bright bearer of the Silmaril.

Jakob Grimm compared Earendil with Odysseus for his voyages and adventures.[4] The same comparison can be made with the Eärendil of Tolkien's works. His penetration of a western Evernight is comparable to Odysseus' journey to the underworld outside the Pillars of Hercules. Eärendil's arrival at Elvenhome, driven by a supernatural wind, is similar to Odysseus' arrival at the Land of the Lotus-Eaters to which hostile winds carried him.

The *Prose Edda* contains another story of Earendil in which the god Thór plays a major part. When Thór fought the boastful giant Hrungnir, he killed the giant with his hammer, but was left with part of the giant's weapon, a whetstone, lodged in his head. Thór employed a seeress, Gróa ("Grow-

[4] Grimm, vol. I, p. 374.

ing" or "Grass-green"), to sing spells that would remove the stone. In repayment, Thór interrupted her singing to give her the good news that her husband, Earendil, would soon be home. Thór had recently carried Earendil out of Giantland in a basket. As they crossed the river Élivágar, Earendil's toe froze, and Thór threw it up in the sky where it became the star Earendil. (Jakob Grimm tentatively identified this star as the morning star.) Because of the interruption, Grôa's spell was never completed, and Thór was often depicted with a piece of whetstone embedded in his head.[5]

Although Tolkien's story differs considerably from the Scandinavian accounts, he depicted Eärendil as the mythic mariner and the morning star. He also made use of the Teutonic belief that stars were jewels in the sky and of the ancient symbolism of the star as the token of hope and guidance.

Another important figure among the Elves was Galadriel, the Lady of Lórien, a typical mythic Elf-queen. She was tall, noble, and fair, and her voice was musical and low. She dressed in white, and her hair was golden, a color rare among Elves. Like Varda, Galadriel was given far more importance than her lord, Celeborn. Most significantly, she was the bearer of one of the Elven Rings.

Galadriel is comparable to Berhta ("Bright"), Holda, and all the other women in white in Teutonic mythology who were associated with wells, spun and wove, and gave gifts that turned to gold.[6] Galadriel's fountain, from which water came in which visions could be seen, is similar to the wishing-wells in which people used to give sacrifices in return for blessings

---

[5] Davidson, *Scandinavian Mythology*, p. 60.
[6] Grimm, vol. II, p. 965.

and visions of the future. It also recalls the magic wells through which children fell into fairyland or Dame Holda's country.

Weaving, such as Galadriel and her maidens did for the Fellowship, was traditionally the prerogative of Elves, as smithcraft was of Dwarves. The women of white in Teutonic myth were always weavers, perhaps in the tradition of the Fates and Norns who spun and wove destiny. The grey fabric of Lórien, that camouflaged the wearer, recalls the cloaks of invisibility that Elves sometimes wore in folk tales.[7]

When Galadriel gave gifts to the Company of the Ring, she was reflecting an action traditional to the Teutonic women in white. In the folk tales, the gifts these women gave were usually something valueless, like wood chips, which, when the recipient reached home, were found to have turned to gold. Comparably, some of Galadriel's gifts, although valuable in themselves, turned out to be unexpectedly important. Legolas shot the winged steed of a Nazgûl with his bow from Lórien, Pippin's brooch aided his rescuers, Frodo's star-glass drove back Shelob, and the Elven-cloaks hid the Company time and again.

Galadriel is not only like the women in white, but her swan-boat associates her with the magical white swan-maidens of Teutonic mythology. The swan-maidens also spun, were associated with fountains, and wore magic rings which gave them their swan shape. The Old English word for swan, *ælfet*, indicates a relationship between swans and Elves, for which one Old English word was *alf*. The swan's supernatural appearance was enhanced by its beauty, ghostly color, and muteness.[8]

[7] *Ibid.*, p. 465.
[8] *Ibid.*, p. 444.

When Galadriel offered the farewell chalice to the Fellowship, she was comparable to the Valkyries with their mead
horns, the Grail-Messenger damsels of Arthurian legend, and
the prototypes of both, the Celtic goddesses who presided over
cauldrons of plenty — all supernatural women who offered
divine refreshment and were concerned with the otherworld.
Galadriel's song discloses that she too was concerned with the
Blessed Realm. Though she had little hope of reaching the
Undying Lands, she hoped or guessed that if the quest suc-
ceeded, the Ring-bearer would be permitted to reach the
Uttermost West.

Thranduil's Sylvan Elves, living in gloomy Mirkwood, seem
more insubstantial and more like spirits than the majestic Elves
of Rivendell, Lórien, and the Grey Havens. This is evident in
their ghostly hunting parties with dim horns blowing in the
dusk, the merry feasts from which they disappeared in an
instant if a stranger entered their circles, and their subterranean
fortress with magic doors.

This magic-doored fortress under a hill is like the dwellings
of the Irish Sidhe, who often inhabited hollow hills. Thranduil's Elves were as isolated from men as the Sidhe; they
seldom strayed out of Mirkwood and men seldom strayed in.
However, the general description of the Sylvan Elves is like
that of the Sidhe: remote, immortal, and invested with magic
powers, but not with the power and majesty the Sidhe had
had as the old gods of Ireland.

In contrast, Glorfindel, the Elf of Elrond's household who
helped drive off the Black Riders at the Ford of Bruinen, is a
good example of the Elf as a god. Most of his attributes are
those of gods of the young sun. His white horse, Asfaloth, is
a typical steed of the sun. He also had the golden hair with

which the young sun is always portrayed. Most sunlike of all, he was seen by Frodo as radiant with power. This radiance is comparable to that in the description of the Scandinavian god Balder, traditionally associated with the young sun. Balder was "so fair of face and so shining that a light went forth from him."[9] This is not to say that Glorfindel was modeled after Balder or any specific deity, but that his radiance and power to combat evil seem less like Elven magic than like the forces of the old gods.

The story of half-Elven Arwen and mortal Aragorn is a curious one. The theme of the love of mortals for women from the otherworld is common in folk tales, particularly in Irish tradition. Such marriages seldom come to good, and even Arwen and Elessar's reign together for six-score years ended in tragedy. In the usual formula, the Elvish bride laid down a prohibition which her husband accidentally broke so that the bride disappeared forever. The turn of Tolkien's story, in which the Elf-bride renounced immortality completely and died alone, is unique. It recalls Tolkien's postulation in "On Fairy-Stories": that Elves would write fairy tales for themselves, not based, as ours are, on the escape from death, but upon the escape from deathlessness.

The symbol of the immortal Elves, as seen in Eregion, the deserted land where the Noldor had lived west of Moria, was, appropriately, the holly. Hollin, the name for Eregion in Common Speech, is Middle English for holly. In Celtic mythology the holly was acclaimed King of the Forest Trees. As the medieval "Holly-Tree Carol" declares, "Of all the trees that are in the wood, the holly bears the crown." Its

[9] Frazer, *The Golden Bough*, p. 819.

evergreen leaves are as appropriate a symbol of immortality for Elves as for Christians, and throughout Celtic mythology, the one quality that is consistently pointed out about Elvish folk is their immortality and their rule of immortal realms of the ever-young.

THE DWARVES

The Dwarves of Middle-earth were short, stocky, bearded, subterranean people, skilled in stone and metalwork, masters of strange powers, secretive and long-lived. They had their own language and folkways and followed their own calendar.

In Teutonic myth, Dwarves were smiths and miners in caverns and mountains, but not in the underworld itself. They were ugly, dark, and misshapen, unlike the beautiful light-elves. Dwarves reached maturity in three years and by the age of seven were greybeards.[1] Dwarves had kings who fashioned magnificent underground chambers for themselves, comparable to the realm of Moria and the Kingdom under the Mountain at Erebor in Tolkien's works.

Where Elves were weavers, Dwarves were said to be smiths. The smithcraft at which the Dwarves were adept was not only a useful art, but was held by the ancients and tribal peoples to be sacred and magical. This was not only because of the vital importance of the craft, but because of its close association with the revered metal, iron.[2]

Often smithwork was the prerogative of the shaman. This was the case in ancient Europe and more recently in Africa. The Fans of West Africa, for example, allowed only their

[1] Grimm, *Teutonic Mythology*, vol. II, p. 448.
[2] MacCana, *Celtic Mythology*, pp. 35–36.

chief, who was also a medicine man, to take part in this sacred occupation.[3]

Smiths were also particularly revered by the Celts. In Ireland, smiths were credited with having supernatural powers and with being spell-masters into comparatively recent times. The old Irish smith-god was Goibhniu, who made unfailing weapons. As Gobán Saor (Gobán the Wright) he appears in numerous folk tales as a master smith and builder with a vast fund of lore coupled with a ready wit.

The Dwarves of Teutonic legend were also such skilled miners that it was considered a good omen for human miners to encounter Dwarves underground. This was because the clever Dwarves could be counted on only to mine where there were valuable metals and precious stones.

The Dwarves were also held to be expert craftsmen. The rare and often supernatural quality of the Dwarves' craftsmanship is often alluded to in Tolkien's works. The Dwarves' works ranged from the Dale-made toys at Bilbo's birthday party to the traceried architecture of Moria.

Dwarves were often referred to as craftsmen in Teutonic mythology. The Scandinavian goddess Freyja was indebted to Dwarves for the creation of her golden necklace, Brisingamen.[4] Dwarves also produced the magic fetter with which the wolf Fenrir was bound. The fetter was made of six impossible things, including the breath of a fish and the sound of a cat running.[5]

In the *Prose Edda* there is an account of how Dwarvish craftsmen made the most precious possessions of the Teutonic

[3] Frazer, *The Golden Bough*, p. 99.
[4] Davidson, *Scandinavian Mythology*, p. 89.
[5] Tonnelat, "Teutonic Mythology," *New Larousse Encyclopedia of Mythology*, pp. 252–297.

gods in a competition arranged by the god Loki. Loki, with
characteristic mischief, had cut off the hair of Thór's wife Sif.
Thór would have killed Loki instantly if Loki had not arranged for two Dwarves to replace Sif's hair with tresses of
real gold. At the same time, the Dwarf smiths also made
Skidbladnir, Frey's expandable, swift ship, and Gungnir,
Odin's spear. Loki then arranged for two more Dwarves to
compete with the first pair. The latter two won. They produced Goldbristles, Frey's brilliant golden boar that could run
over land or sea faster than a horse, Draupnir, Odin's treasure-
breeding ring, and Mjolnir, Thór's famous hammer.[6]

In Icelandic myth, Dwarves had an ignominious origin.
When the first being, Ymir the giant, had been killed by Odin
and his brothers, his body became the world. In the vast
corpse, grubs began to grow which the gods transformed into
Dwarves. Born of and living in Ymir's body at their origin,
they continued in this way after the giant's body became the
world, when they lived in caverns and mines.[7]

The Dwarves in *The Lord of the Rings* lived to a great age.
They were born of Dwarf-women, but seldom, for there were
few women among them. According to the *Prose Edda*, however, new Dwarves were formed of earth by mysterious
princes named Môtsognir and Durinn, for there were no
women among the Dwarves to bear them children.[8]

It is probably from the above myth that Tolkien chose the
name Durin for the longfather of the Dwarves of Middle-
earth. Most of the Dwarf names that Tolkien used were from
the *Prose Edda* or were in the style of those names, which
often rhymed. In the Edda, these names had the following

6 Davidson, p. 70.
7 Tonnelat, p. 249.
8 Snorri Sturluson, *The Prose Edda*, p. 34.

forms (translations by Young are given when available): Dvalin ("One lying in a trance"), Nár ("Corpse"), Ori ("Raging one"), Ganndálf ("Sorcerer-elf"), Thorin ("Bold one"), and Fundin ("Found one"). Mention was also made of Náin, Dáin, Bifur, Báfur, Bömbör, Dóri, Nori, Oin, Fili, Kili, and Thrór. Eikinskjaldi ("With-oak-shield") is mentioned as a Dwarf that came from Svarin's grave-mound.[9]

Certain Dwarf names such as Nár and Náin are related to the word *nair* which was applied to the deathly pale or ghostly members of the Dwarf-people.[10] This suggests that to some degree Dwarves were considered to be spirits of the dead, although this is not indicated of Tolkien's Dwarves, who were mortal although they possessed supernatural powers.

The name of Glóin's son, Gimli, of the Company of the Ring, has its source in another part of the *Prose Edda*. *Gimlé* is the name of the most beautiful hall in the heavens, brighter than the sun. The name itself means "Lee-of-Flame" and may be related to the German word for heaven, *Himmel*. This heaven is supposed to endure the destruction of heaven and earth and become the eternal dwelling of righteous men. Until then it is the abode of the light-elves.[11]

The word Dwarf itself comes from the Old English *Dwearg*.[12] The standard English plural for Dwarf is Dwarfs. However, Tolkien suggests that if *dwarf* had been a commonly used word, the plural would have become *dwarrows* or *dwerrows*.[13] As a compromise, Tolkien uses the plural *Dwarves* for its parallel construction to the plural *Elves*.

The Dwarves of Middle-earth were secretive and never

[9] *Ibid.*, pp. 41–42.
[10] Grimm, p. 445.
[11] Snorri Sturluson, p. 47.
[12] Grimm, p. 447.
[13] Tolkien, *The Return of the King*, p. 415.

allowed their real names to be known: their secret names were not even recorded on their tombs. Comparable beliefs in the importance of names is worldwide. Many tribal groups consider their names to be parts of themselves which need to be guarded. For this reason such people often bear two names, one for casual use and one that is either a total secret or is used guardedly. The purpose in this is to prevent the real name from coming under the influence of destructive forces, such as the wiles of a sorcerer or the malice of an evil spirit. These practices are an example of the belief in a separable soul, the name in this case being the repository of the soul, vulnerable to magic forces.[14] A characteristic example of the theme of a magic secret name is recorded in an Egyptian myth. Isis sought the secret powers of Ra, the sun god, which she knew were resident in his secret name. She magically produced a serpent from Ra's saliva, and when the serpent bit him, she refused to cure the wound until she had obtained the secret of Ra's name, and with it his power.[15]

Another important Dwarf belief recorded in *The Lord of the Rings* is an echo of many Celtic and Teutonic hero stories. The Dwarves believed that their ancestor, Durin the Deathless, slept in his tomb and returned to the living in the form of successors who resembled him and bore his name. The comparable belief that heroes sometimes sleep in caverns under mountains and issue forth in times of need is widespread. Such legends are commonly repeated about Odin, Sigurd, Arthur, Merlin, Charlemagne, and Frederic Barbarossa.[16]

Sometimes the Teutons saw Dwarves as a shy, downtrodden,

[14] Frazer, pp. 284–289.
[15] Viaud, "Egyptian Mythology," *New Larousse Encyclopedia of Mythology*, p. 19.
[16] Grimm, vol. I, p. 394.

afflicted heathen race, shrinking from men and distrustful of modern improvements. The Dwarves were particularly disapproving of churches, bells, pounding machinery for ore, the clearing of forests, and agriculture. Many tales describe the efforts of Dwarves to leave the regions where these revolutionary ideas were being introduced.[17]

TOM BOMBADIL AND GOLDBERRY

Tom Bombadil is a character like Puck or Pan, a nature god in diminished form, half humorous, half divine. His divinity is seen in that he was immortal, oldest, and fatherless. He was master of plant and animal life and of the earth itself in a circumscribed area including the Old Forest and the Barrow Downs. There he easily escaped natural and supernatural dangers and helped the hobbits to escape them as well.

It is emphasized that Bombadil was his own master, and master, though not owner, of the lands around him. Within his borders he was secure from outside influence. Even the pervasive magic of the Ring had no hold on him.

Bombadil's power lay primarily in his unquenchable gaiety and in his sung spells. These simple, persuasive spells saved him from all the snares set for him in the poem "The Adventures of Tom Bombadil."[1] With such a simple spell, Frodo summoned Tom to rescue the hobbits from the Barrow-wight, one of the worst dangers they ever faced. Some of Bombadil's spells were, in fact, counterspells; at least two of the enemies in his land, Old Man Willow and the Barrow-wights, used spells themselves.

[17] *Ibid.*, vol. II, p. 459.
[1] Tolkien, "The Adventures of Tom Bombadil," *The Tolkien Reader.*

Peculiarly, a fragment of a specific Teutonic myth is associated with Bombadil. A sequence out of the *Volsungsaga* is casually referred to in the poem "Bombadil goes Boating" in *The Adventures of Tom Bombadil*. It is tossed off as a taunt made by Bombadil to an otter, and indicates the degree to which myth penetrated even Tolkien's most frivolous works:

> "I'll give your otter-fell to Barrow-wights. They'll
>   taw you!
> Then smother you in gold rings! Your mother if she
>   saw you,
> she'd never know her son, unless 'twas by a whisker.
> Nay, don't tease old Tom, until you be far brisker!"[2]

The reference is to Hreidmar's son Otter, who could take on an otter's form. It was in this form that Otter was killed by the god Loki, who later took lodging in Hreidmar's home and boasted of his catch. Hreidmar demanded that the otter-skin be entirely filled and covered with gold in compensation. To fulfill this demand, Loki and Odin, who was accompanying him, took the Dwarf Andvari's gold hoard. When the skin had been filled and the pelt covered with gold, one whisker remained visible. To complete the agreement, Odin was forced to relinquish Andvari's treasure-breeding ring. It was as well that he did so: the Dwarf had placed a curse on the ring, which brought destruction to all its owners.[3]

When Bombadil was asked who he was, he replied enigmatically, "Don't you know my name yet? That's the only answer." The name Bombadil seems to incorporate Middle English words for "humming" and "hidden," reflect-

[2] *Ibid.*
[3] Snorri Sturluson, *The Prose Edda*, pp. 111–112.

ing Tom's secrecy and tunefulness. Bombadil's name among
the Dwarves, Forn, is associated by Grimm with the words
"old" and "sorcery." Orald, his name among northern men,
is Old English for "very old, ancient, original." His Sindarin
name, Iarwain Ben-adar, may mean "oldest, fatherless."

The great antiquity alluded to by Bombadil's names is appropriate to his being a nature divinity or spirit. The belief in
forest or nature gods naturally precedes that of harvest spirits,
as forest gods were worshiped before the evolution of agriculture.[4]

While Bombadil was a forest god, Goldberry was as un-
mistakably a watersprite. She was a nixie, the Riverwoman's
daughter, discovered by Tom among the pools of the mysterious Withywindle. As all the other creatures Tom met in "The
Adventures of Tom Bombadil" were dangerous, so Goldberry
must have been. She had the allure of the Undine, the Lorelei,
and the Siren to lead folk into the depths. In the end, Tom
caught her instead and made her his bride. In the last line of
the poem, Goldberry sits combing her yellow hair. This is not
the simple domestic action that it seems, but is the characteristic pose of all types of watersprites.

In *The Fellowship of the Ring*, Goldberry no longer appears dangerous, but is a modest and beautiful hostess. She
remains a water spirit, but the water she represents is no longer
the treacherous Withywindle, but the rains and streams that
replenish plant life. She is the protectress of flowers, guarding
water lilies and wearing garlands. Her songs are about the
beauties of nature; they are not the alluring, fatal music common to all water spirits. Her dresses, blue and green shot with
gold and silver, are water-colored. They recall the wet skirts

[4] Frazer, *The Golden Bough*, p. 441.

and aprons by which nixies are traditionally recognized in Teutonic mythology.[5]

Bombadil and Goldberry are undisguised personifications of land untouched by humans, underlaid by a hidden but potent power, representing both the danger of wild land and its potential to serve man. But Bombadil and Goldberry's outstanding characteristic is independence; they will neither frighten nor serve, though they may awe or aid chance travelers. Neither will they be daunted or served by others. Like their land that existed long ages before the coming of man, and remained unchanged after the departure of man from the North Kingdom, they are their own masters.

THE ENTS

Both good and evil giants existed in myth, ranging from helpful, harmless creatures like larger versions of household and farmyard elves to hideous ogres, eaters of man-flesh. Tolkien differentiated between these two natures, giving the name Troll to the harmful giants and the name Ent to the benign guardians of the forest who were dangerous but not evil.

Ent is an Old English word meaning giant. Among supernatural creatures, Tolkien's Ents are most like the huge, wild, hairy woodsprites of Teutonic myth. These, like giants, left seat- and hand-prints in stone and were vastly strong and old. Like Ents, the woodsprites were guardians of the woods who hated treecutters.[1] In character, the Ents resemble the ancient fallen race of wise and faithful giants whose passing was spoken of regretfully in the *Prose Edda.*[2]

[5] Grimm, *Teutonic Mythology*, vol. II, p, p. 491.
[1] Grimm, *Teutonic Mythology*, vol. II, p. 553.
[2] *Ibid.*, p. 529.

Giants were old nature gods and, like Ents, were considered
the oldest of all creatures. The giant Ymir, according to the
Prose Edda, was the first being, formed from melting rime and
hoarfrost.[3]

It is curious that the ancient, unwieldy Ents were credited
with having beautiful, graceful Entwives. However, in myth,
this same contrast is often seen between grim giants and their
beautiful wives and daughters. Among the beautiful giantesses
was Gerd, the radiant daughter of the giant Gymir. She was
so beautiful that she won the love of the Scandinavian god
Frey.[4] In the Arthurian Cycle, Carl (Churl) of Carlisle, a man
under an enchantment that gave him the form of a giant, had
a beautiful wife and daughter. Sir Gawain freed Carl by
beheading him and won the daughter for his bride.

The separation of the Ents and Entwives, each loving a
particular type of land, recalls that of the Scandinavian god
Njörd from his wife Skadi, daughter of the giant Thjazi.
Each tried to live in the other's homeland, but Njörd protested
that the song of the seaside swans was more beautiful to him
than the howling of the mountain wolves at Skadi's home at
Thrymheim ("Stormhome"). She in turn complained that on
the shore where Njörd lived, the screaming seagulls kept her
awake.[5] Like the Ents and Entwives, Njörd and Skadi separated and went to live in their favorite lands.

The Entwives, who cherished domestic plants and taught
men their uses, are characteristic of goddesses such as Demeter
and Ceres, who gave mankind the gift of agriculture. Like
these goddesses, the Entwives were described in terms of domestic vegetation, with corn-colored hair and apple-red cheeks.

[3] *Ibid.*, p. 532.
[4] *Ibid.*, p. 530.
[5] Tonnelat, "Teutonic Mythology," *New Larousse Encyclopedia of Mythology*, p. 270.

The Ents are a good example of Tolkien's making of an imaginative extrapolation from the most sparse accounts in myth. As with the Woses, he began with hardly more than the name, in this case *ent*, the generic Old English term for giants, and vague mythic references to manlike, treelike guardian spirits of forests. To these he added character, a history, the tragedy of the Entwives, and special powers. In spite of their unprepossessing appearance, the Ents have been invested with some elements of dignity and pathos: they are a forgotten race remet shortly before they are to vanish.

SAURON

Sauron, the Enemy of the free peoples for two ages of the world, was almost certainly an evil Vala. He was described as the servant of the Great Enemy, Morgoth, in the First Age. Sauron escaped the downfall of Morgoth's fortress, Thangorodrim, and carried on his master's work of corruption in Middle-earth.

Sauron, as an evil god or angel, is not a typical character of pre-Christian European myth. The concept, basic to *The Lord of the Rings*, of dualism between good and evil evolved from Persian Zendic concepts which prevailed in the Near East and reached Europe most fully developed in Christianity. Before the adoption of this dualism, gods such as Odin, Loki, and Hel, although associated with evil, occupied an ambivalent position in the minds of their worshipers. It was believed that the arbitrary bestowal or withdrawal of the gods' favor caused the unpredictability of human fate.

While, to the reader, Sauron usually represents the modern concept of an evil power, most of his specific characteristics are those of pagan gods. This combination of views is itself characteristic of myth. Many of the pagan gods associated with death or arbitrary betrayal were identified with the devil after the introduction of Christianity. Like the devil, Sauron could corrupt, work magic, and create illusions, but could not take part in material creation. Like the pagan gods, Sauron had supernatural powers concerning the sun, the dead, and divine warfare. Like rulers and sorcerers in pagan myth, Sauron had a separable soul which forms the crux of the entire work.

It may seem incongruous to identify Tolkien's Dark Lord with gods of the sun, but Sauron shared with them the characteristic of physical as well as moral darkness. Several solar gods, including Lugh, Balar, and Odin, were similarly dark or associated with darkness as well as with death and cruelty. Sauron himself also had power over the sun, the power of eclipsing it with the volcanic smokes of Mount Doom and with the veils of darkness that issued from Barad-dûr.

Sauron is also analogous to solar gods in that he is described as firy-eyed. The recurring vision of Sauron's glowing evil eye is always discussed in the singular, as if he had only one eye or one evil eye. Several Celtic and Teutonic solar gods were identified by a single firy eye representing the sun.

Two Celtic solar gods, Lugh and Balar, were adversaries. Lugh the Longhanded was a youthful, warlike god who was supposed to have gone "around the Men of Erin one-footed and with one eye."[1] Lugh also produced a magic mist of gloom with the fountain of dark blood that welled from his head in his battle frenzy.[2] This mist parallels Sauron's obscuring smokes and mists in Mordor. Balar was the god of

[1] Loomis, *Celtic Myth and Arthurian Romance*, p. 121.
[2] *Ibid.*, p. 49.

the Fomorians, the traditional adversaries of the Tuatha Dé Danann, the old Irish gods. He was called Balar of the Baleful Eye because he had one huge eye which could destroy armies with its glance. Lugh killed Balar with a slingstone which drove the baleful eye through the back of Balar's head where it destroyed his own forces.[3]

Sauron also resembles a curious Welsh mythic figure, the Black Oppressor. The Black Oppressor was described in *The Mabinogion* as a black, one-eyed man who had lost one eye to the Black Serpent of the Carn. Both the Oppressor and serpent were vanquished by Peredur (Percival).[4]

In all mythology, Sauron is most similar to the Scandinavian god Odin. Odin, like Lugh and Balar, seems to have been a solar god, with a single firy eye above his blue cloak representing the sun in the heavens. Odin was said to have had only one eye because he paid the other to Mimir, guardian of the spring of wisdom, for a drink of the water of knowledge. Among Odin's titles were *Bileyg*, "One whose eye deceives him" (One-eyed), and *Báleyg*, "Flame-eyed."

The name Odin itself seems to mean "Frenzy" or "Rage." This name refers to Odin's great gift to his followers, one which Sauron provided as well: the gift of ecstatic frenzy in battle. Odin's great weapon was the opposite, the "army-fetter," *herfjöturr*, a spell of paralyzing panic which he could send out against warriors in the same way that the Nazgûl radiated a panic spell. Odin, again like Sauron, did not go out to battle, as, for example, did Thór, but wielded his powers from a distance.[5]

There is no doubt that Tolkien's parallels between Sauron

---

[3] MacCana, *Celtic Mythology*, p. 59.
[4] *The Mabinogion*, p. 201.
[5] Tolkien, *Tree and Leaf*, p. 31.

and Odin were conscious ones. When Tolkien mentioned Odin in his essay "On Fairy-Stories,"[6] he referred to him as "the Necromancer," as he did Sauron, and called him "the Lord of the Slain," paralleling the title "Lord of the Rings." Sauron has affinities with other gods of the dead and of the underworld. His realm was named Mordor, meaning "Black Country" in Sindarin and "Murder," "Torment," and "Mortal Sin" in Old English. A part of that realm bore the name Udûn, which means "Hell," probably in Sindarin. Sauron's followers were demons, wraiths, and other malignant supernatural creatures such as those that people mythic underworlds. By the Third Age, Sauron was himself one of the living dead, destroyed in the downfall of Númenor and vanquished again by the Last Alliance, with the Ring that gave him strength lopped from his black hand.

That Sauron is described as black is in accordance with the descriptions of several gods of the dead. The devil was often depicted as black, as was the Greek underworld god Pluto. India's black death-goddess Kali takes her name from her color. The primary Irish god of the dead, later associated with the devil, was named Donn, meaning "the Brown" or "Dark One." Hel, Loki's daughter to whom the dead were said to go, was believed to be black or half black and half pale. Similarly the Greek Furies were described as black or half pale, half dark.[7]

Sauron also resembled necromancers, who were believed to have control over weather. At the height of his power, Sauron directed storms, clouds, and volcanic activity. The control of weather is traditionally the prerogative of magicians, as Frazer

---

[6] Tonnelat, "Teutonic Mythology," *New Larousse Encyclopedia of Mythology*, p. 254.

[7] Grimm, *Teutonic Mythology*, vol. III, p. 993.

discusses at length in *The Golden Bough*.[8] This power, when
exercised for the good, was essential to the lives of tribal
peoples, and sorcerers believed to provide it were elevated to
the position of chief or king.

The most significant element of Sauron's story, and that
which establishes the mythic genre of *The Lord of the Rings*,
is the One Ring. The basic irony is that Sauron should have
bound up so much of his power in a ring that could, and did,
escape him and bring about his destruction. However, this
ill-advised action is taken by numerous sorcerers and kings in
myths and folk tales. The basis of this theme is the belief in a
soul separable from the living body.

It was a widespread belief, and remains so among tribal
peoples, that the soul or life-force can leave the living body
and be confined in an external object (in the way that Sauron
secreted much of his power in the Ring). Some tribal peoples,
in time of danger, hide representations of their souls in safe
places, deeming that as long as their souls are protected, their
bodies will go unscathed. A similar practice is that of wearing
amulets believed to contain one's soul.

In folk tales, the theme of the external soul follows this
general format: a king or sorcerer has his soul confined in a
special object which is either secret or hidden where it cannot
be reached by normal means. A hero learns the secret and is
aided, often by an animal, in locating the object. The hero
destroys the object and with it the owner of the soul.[9] The
story of the One Ring follows the same basic pattern. The
Ring was the repository of Sauron's strength and maintained
the cohesive force by which his works were sustained. Bilbo
found the Ring where it had been dropped by the beastlike
Gollum. The powers of the Ring were secret, and not dis-

8 Frazer, *The Golden Bough*, Chapter V.
9 Grimm, vol. I, p. 312.

covered for seventy-seven years. Frodo took the Ring into the apparently impregnable land of Mordor, guided by the creature, Gollum, and destroyed together the Ring, its owner, and his fortress.

Classical mythology contains examples of external souls. In a Greek myth, the life and throne of Nisus, King of Megara, were dependent on a lock of purple or golden hair that grew at the center of his scalp. His daughter, Scylla, cut off the lock, killing him out of love for her father's enemy, Minos of Crete.

In another Greek myth, the hero Meleager's fate was bound to that of a firebrand that his mother had snatched from the hearth at the time of his birth because of a prophecy that he would live only as long as it remained unburned. Later, in vengeance for the slaying of her brothers, she returned the brand to the flames and her son died in agony.[10]

In the Russian folk tale immortalized by Stravinski's ballet *The Firebird*, the soul of the sorcerer, Koschei the Deathless, was hidden in an egg. A supernatural firebird helped a prince to obtain this egg. When this was found and broken, the sorcerer and his demons were destroyed, and a princess he had held in captivity was released.[11]

The story of the Tartar hero Kök Chan describes the effects of a separable soul returned to the body in time of need. Half the strength of Kök Chan resided in a gold ring which he gave to a maiden for safekeeping. When the hero wrestled with an enemy he could not kill, the maiden dropped the ring in his mouth, giving him the power to overcome his foe.[12] The details of this story parallel Sauron's story closely. In both it is a gold ring that holds supernatural strength, although both

---

[10] Frazer, p. 774.
[11] *Ibid.*, p. 777.
[12] *Ibid.*, p. 783.

characters have some strength apart from their rings. If Sauron had been reunited with his Ring, as was Kök Chan, he would certainly have overcome his enemies.

It is significant that Tolkien turned to a mythological theme as pervasive as that of the sorcerer with his separable soul to provide the central problem of *The Lord of the Rings*. Its theme immediately establishes the mythic basis of the work, and classifies the essential quest that it describes. Some authorities deny that this is a quest at all. It would be more accurate to say that it is the quest inverted. The classic quest is a search for the token of the attainment of Good. *The Lord of the Rings* is an odyssey to reject a token, thereby achieving denial of Evil. As has been demonstrated, the mythic formula by which this is done is an essential and universal one, as basic and vital as the Quest. Tolkien's twist to the formula is a telling one. The evil token, the "soul of the sorcerer," is, as the story begins, already in the hands of the hero, unrecognized, but potent. The hero's search is for the place to destroy the token, a place which, ironically, lies within the sorcerer's stronghold. The message is clear: one does not need to make a quest to find evil; the struggle is to deny Evil itself, which can be done only when Evil is fully recognized.

THE EVIL CREATURES

Among the evil peoples of Middle-earth, Tolkien placed special emphasis on four types of beings which have significant mythic parallels. These are the Nazgûl, the Balrog, the Trolls, and the Orcs.

The Nazgûl were the most effectively pitted against the Company of the Ring. They wore the Nine Rings and rode both earth and sky to do Sauron's bidding.

Of all the rings ruled by Sauron, only the Nine Rings worked fully to his purpose. They were given to mortal kings of Númenorean descent as a promise of power and immortality, but they brought enslavement and doom. The kings were bound by the force of the One Ring and faded into invisible wraiths clothed in the trappings of the real world. In the Black Speech these spirits were called Nazgûl, meaning Ringwraiths. Only Frodo, half in the wraith-world himself (wearing the Ring on Weathertop and overcome by his wound at the Ford of Bruinen), saw the Nazgûl in their human forms, old and haggard, helmed with silver, white-haired and keen-eyed.

The leader of the Nazgûl, the Witch-king of Angmar, waged war upon the Dúnedain of Arnor until their kingdom was ended and they were reduced to a tribe of Rangers. Eärnur, the Captain of Gondor who later became Gondor's last king, came north with a large fleet, but was too late to save the last king of Arnor. However, Eärnur drove the armies of the Witch-king out of Fornost and cut off the Witch-king's retreat to Carn Dûm in Angmar.

At the end of the battle, Glorfindel, an Elf of Elrond's house, made the prophecy to Eärnur that the Witch-king would never fall by the hand of man. This prophecy was like many deceptive prophecies in legend. The most familiar are those made to Macbeth by the three weird sisters, implying his invincibility but actually outlining a strange doom. The Witch-king lived on for centuries, but he was destroyed within the framework of the prophecy — at the hands of Éowyn, a woman, and Meriadoc, a hobbit.

The Nazgûl adhere to the pattern in myth of the vengeful dead who seek to carry off the living. The fear of the vengeance of the dead is one of the oldest concepts of myth and plays a part in the beliefs of even the earliest tribal

peoples. What seem to be efforts to placate and restore life
to the dead can be seen even in Paleolithic burials. Man seems
always to have had a universal fear of the wraiths of the dead
and to have gone to great lengths to keep the dead from in-
truding into the world of the living.

Similarly, the black horses of the Nine are like the black
steeds that are traditionally believed to carry off the damned.[1]
The Nazgûl's Black Breath is like the blasting breath of
witches, as much feared for its damage as the witches' evil
eyes.[2]

Most significantly, while Sauron resembles Odin, the Nazgûl resemble Odin's messengers, his most trusted champions,
the *einherjar*. The *einherjar* were depicted as men with
helmets that had beaks like those of eagles and horns like a
bull's. Like the Nine, the *einherjar* went out to the battlefield
in Odin's place to determine the fate of the mortal warriors.
They chose those who were to return with them to Valhalla,
as the Ringwraiths had planned to convey Frodo's enslaved
spirit to Mordor after they had wounded him on Weathertop.
The *einherjar* were destined to lead the host of the noble dead
warriors whom Odin had mustered for the final battle of
Ragnarök. In the same way, the Ringwraiths led the Orcs and
evil peoples for Sauron in the final battles of the War of the
Ring. The Nazgûl were destroyed in the firy ruin of Mount
Doom, as it must have been thought the *einherjar* would
perish in the flames that were to destroy the world.[3]

Although they play a lesser part than most other creatures
under Sauron's sway, one group of evil beings appears in

[1] Grimm, *Teutonic Mythology*, vol. III, p. 994.
[2] *Ibid.*, p. 1099.
[3] Davidson, *Scandinavian Mythology*, p. 38.

Tolkien's works unchanged from the pattern they traditionally follow in myth. These are the Trolls, who, arising from the same lore as the Ents which have become uniquely Tolkien's, are still wholly different from them. As the Ents partook of all that was benevolent and treelike in the myths about giants, so Tolkien's Trolls took on all the characteristics that were malevolent and stonelike.

In Teutonic myth, many giants were made of stone, were animated stones, were part stone, were old as stone, were turned to stone, or bore stone weapons. The bearing of stone weapons reinforces the giants' antiquity: giants were stone-age beings indeed, and no iron sword could wound them.[4]

Giants dreaded daylight, because if surprised by daybreak they became stone.[5] This was the fate of the Trolls that captured Bilbo and his companions in *The Hobbit*. The story implies that the Trolls were animated stone, and one ray of daylight was enough to return them to immobility.

The theme is common — for example, the giant Hrimgerd was one of many who, overcome by daylight, became stone. The same fate overcame the Dwarf Alvis. He had come to Thór to ask for the god's daughter's hand in marriage. Instead, Thór tricked Alvis by riddling with him all night about the names of things in the languages of men, gods, giants, Elves, and Dwarves. This kept the unwary Dwarf talking until sunrise which turned him to stone.[6]

This theme may have its origin in the anxiety felt toward the dark in times when nothing could be seen beyond the short range of a torch's light. Anything could conceivably be abroad, making the night noises, and since these unknown

[4] Grimm, vol. II, p. 533.
[5] *Ibid.*, p. 551.
[6] *Elder Edda*, pp. 79–83.

things were never seen in the daytime, it may have seemed reasonable to believe that daylight was dangerous to them.

There were other ways of transforming giants into stone. Numerous tales of King Olaf the Holy, the early Christian king of Norway, tell of rhyming giants and giantesses into stone, each story being illustrated with the appropriate rock formation.[7] Such natural formations in more or less human shape must be an inspiration of many of these stories, just as tales of the effect of giants on the landscape arise from formations resembling giant foot- or hand-prints.

In Norway, on Saint John's Eve (Midsummer Eve), bonfires of nine kinds of wood as well as of toadstools were burned at crossroads. These fires were supposed to overcome the power of Trolls, who, if they were in the vicinity, had to show themselves.[8] It is not unlikely that these fires, which seem to have been built originally to honor and give power to the sun as it reached the summer solstice, were supposed to have an effect like that of sunlight on the unfortunate Trolls. Mistletoe, possibly because it was sacred to the sun, was hung in houses and barns in Sweden to prevent Trolls from harming man or beast.[9]

In another tradition, giants were held responsible for having built ancient ruins. Such buildings were called *eald enta geweorc* in Old English, with the same idea that the Greeks had when they called ancient polygonal masonry "Cyclopean" after the one-eyed giants, the Cyclopes, to whom they attributed that architecture. In view of this, it is not surprising that the old towers beyond the Last Bridge reminded the

[7] Grimm, p. 550.
[8] Frazer, *The Golden Bough*, p. 724.
[9] *Ibid.*, p. 814.

hobbits of Trolls, although the Trolls of Middle-earth did not build.

Giants were considered man-eaters that could smell man-flesh acutely. They were also great drinkers — in fact, the Old Norse *thurs* (giant) is very close to *thhurr* (dry, thirsty).[10] The characteristic cannibalism, gluttony, and thievishness of Teutonic giants can be seen in the Trolls that captured Bilbo and the Dwarves.

The word Troll itself and other words for Trolls give an insight into the original concepts compared with Tolkien's. The Scandinavian word *troll* was a generic term for any supernatural creature, including Dwarves and giants. The Old English word *Eoten*, meaning "giant," also meant "Jutlander," while the Germanic word for giants, *Hune*, also meant "Huns." It is easy to follow the reasoning by which the word for an enemy people became the word for anything huge and savage. Another word for giant, *Lubbe*, is related to the Modern English word "lubber." As will be discussed, giants were often considered to be clumsy, lubberly louts. Torog, Tolkien's Sindarin word for Troll, and Olog-hai, the name in Black Speech for evil, fighting Trolls, share the syllable *og* with Balrog, suggesting the word "ogre," ultimately derived from Orcus, the name of the Roman god of the underworld.

According to Teutonic belief, men were a median between the cunning, diminutive Dwarves and the huge, dull-witted giants. Giants were consistently depicted as easily outwitted. The brave little tailor in the Grimms' fairy tale, who killed "seven at one blow," got the best of two sleeping giants by throwing things at them until they each blamed the other and fought to the death. This was much the same as Gandalf's

[10] Grimm, p. 552.

device for keeping the Trolls in *The Hobbit* fighting until they were overcome by the dawn.

The evil creatures in Tolkien's works occupy the mythological position of the Teutonic giants, Trolls, and demons. They represented the terrifying gods of the underworld and spirits of the terrifying side of nature. In Teutonic myth, giants and Trolls were developed as personifications of natural elements in their most terrifying forms. Aegir and his wife Ran, for example, were Scandinavian giants who represented the violence of the sea. Other giants were responsible for the growls and roars in river chasms, for earthquakes, and for thunderstorms.[11] In *The Hobbit*, the giants who rolled stones about in the storm on the Misty Mountains were of this type.

The parentage and offspring credited to giants in myth indicates the horror with which they were regarded. The fifty giants in the army of Emperor Lucius that rode against King Arthur were engendered by fiends.[12] The Scandinavian god Loki and the giantess Angrboda (Boder of Sorrow) were the parents of the wolf Fenrir, Jörmungand (the Midgard serpent), and Hel, all of whom were adversaries of the gods.[13] In *Beowulf*, giants were held to be among the descendants of Cain.[14] The origin of the Trolls of Middle-earth was also uncompromisingly evil; they were created by the power of Morgoth, the Great Enemy.

As the Trolls of Middle-earth are grim counterfeits of Ents, the numerous, violent Orcs are grotesque parodies of

[11] Tonnelat, "Teutonic Mythology," *New Larousse Encyclopedia of Mythology*, p. 280.
[12] Malory, *Le Morte Darthur*, vol. I, p. 171.
[13] Snorri Sturluson, *The Prose Edda*, p. 56.
[14] *Beowulf*, 106–112.

Elves. In Teutonic mythology both Elves and goblins could be tall or short, beautiful or ugly, good or evil. Tolkien differentiated these characteristics so that Elves in Middle-earth are tall, beautiful, and virtuous, while goblins are short, ugly, and evil.

In *The Lord of the Rings*, Orcs, Trolls, and Balrogs were creations of Morgoth. When Morgoth was thrown down, these creatures scattered throughout Middle-earth and set up strongholds for themselves. The most numerous of these creatures were the Orcs, who were also the most troublesome, if least powerful. They produced little on their own other than devices of war or torture, so they were always in search of plunder or of slaves, who served them both as workers and nourishment. Orcs were enthusiastic fighters, but could not be easily organized. They were treacherous to one another and took poorly to discipline.

The name Orc is significant: both *orc*, the Old English word for demon, and *ogre* are derived from Orcus, the name of the Roman god of the underworld. This is appropriate. The Orcs under Sauron's sway are comparable to the demons of some infernal deity. *Orc* is also the Irish word for pig; the carrion-eating swine were also associated with the underworld in the accounts of such goddesses as Demeter, Persephone, and the Celtic Carridwen. The comparison with swine only begins to suggest the qualities of Tolkien's filthy, demonic, cannibalistic Orcs.

Uruk was the word in the Black Speech for the largest Orcs. In Sindarin Elvish, the word for Orc was *orch* and the plural was *yrch:* all words similar to Orcus. Goblin, the word Tolkien used as a synonym for Orc, is derived, with kobold, from the Greek *kóbalos* (rogue), through the Latin *cobalus* and *gobelinus* to the French *gobelin*, a homesprite.

The goblin in Teutonic myth was sometimes beneficent, while at other times it was the bogy or bugbear that carried off children and led travelers astray.[15] Ogres in folk tales were said to be black, hairy, bristly, and of great stature. Sometimes they were good-natured, more often their wives were so, and protected travelers from their grisly ogre husbands who could smell human flesh acutely and were always eager to gobble up stray adventurers.[16] Among goblins, in contrast to ogres, there were no women, which agrees with Tolkien's account.

A common characteristic of goblins in Teutonic mythology was the horrible laugh with which they celebrated their pranks. This grisly glee was also seen among the Orcs who captured Bilbo and the Dwarves under the Misty Mountains and later hoped to burn them in the forest.

Contrasted with the swarms of stunted, bestial Orcs, the Balrog was a vast, elemental force rivaling Gandalf in supernatural power. The Balrog was a creation of the Great Enemy that escaped to Moria after Morgoth's downfall. When it was unintentionally released from the deeps by the Dwarves, it rose and guarded Moria's East Gate for over two thousand years. In appearance, it was a huge spirit of fire and shadow bearing a flaming sword. It wielded a horrible power that terrified even the Orcs and Trolls that gathered around it.

The Balrog has several parallels with the adversary of the Teutonic gods, Surt ("Swart"). Both were giant figures combining darkness and consuming fire. Each was armed with a flaming sword and each fought on a high frail bridge, breaking it down.

[15] Grimm, p. 502.
[16] Ibid., p. 486.

Surt was one of the primary destructive forces prophesied to appear for Ragnarök, the end of the world. It was believed that Surt would ride with his host over Bifröst, the Rainbow Bridge to Heaven, and destroy it. He would fight against the gods and destroy them, and he would overwhelm the world with fire. It was believed that after the conflagration, the sea would cover the world, but at last the world would rise out of the sea again, renewed, bearing the sons of the old gods, and Balder risen from Hel.[17]

The Balrog's conflict with Gandalf, producing earthquakes and storms among the mountains, reflects the elemental combat of Ragnarök. The outcome is similar as well, with the powerful wizard destroyed in overthrowing his enemy, but returned to life in a higher form.

All the evil creatures that fought in the War of the Ring are comparable to the combatants in the final conflicts at the Twilight of the Gods. It may seem ironic that they include not only the creatures comparable to the demons, giants, and the victor, Surt, who fought against the gods, but also Sauron and the Nazgûl, who resemble the god Odin and his faithful emissaries. However, by the time of the final battle of Ragnarök, Odin, like Sauron, was doomed, and the gods themselves had become corrupt and violent, bringing their fate upon themselves. To some degree this may be the retrospective viewpoint of the myths, as they were recorded at least two centuries after the conversion to Christianity, with an unsympathetic view of the old gods. However, the whole body of Teutonic myth bears out the idea that the gods, especially Odin and Loki, were often treacherous and without honor. The turning point in the fate of the gods came about when Loki arranged

[17] *Ibid.*, p. 814.

the murder of the beloved young god Balder. Loki was bound to stones in punishment, but eventually he broke away and joined the gods' adversaries in revenge against the gods.

As was the War of the Ring, the Twilight of the Gods was portended by omens, dreams, and the appearance of evil creatures. The dawnless day and the great darkness that ushered in the final days of Middle-earth's Third Age reflect the years of darkness and endless winter that preceded Ragnarök. These occurred when a terrible wolf, Loki's grandson, destroyed the sun. The destruction of Mordor in the eruption of the firy mountain is like the ruin of the Teutonic heaven and earth in Surt's flames. Tolkien's interpretation of the destroying fire as volcanic action has been previously suggested as an explanation for myths about Ragnarök. Volcanic activity is common in Iceland, the source of the *Eddas*, and could well have inspired both the mythic cataclysm and Mordor's destruction.

With the destruction of Mordor, most of the Wise and Immortal sought the Undying Lands, and Middle-earth entered a new age, the age of the dominion of man. In the same way, after Ragnarök, the earth rose cleansed from the sea, still crowned by the World Tree, sheltering a mortal man and woman in its branches. In less mythic terms, the defeat of the old gods ushered in a new age of belief in man, not bound by arbitrary fate, but worshiping the Son of Man.

PART
V

THINGS

THINGS

THROUGHOUT Tolkien's works, a number of things are given special significance. Four categories of things that are important both in Tolkien's writing and in mythology are discussed in this section. They are dragons, Rings of Power, weapons, and barrows.

Dragons have been listed as things, not beings, because all the other beings of Middle-earth are anthropomorphic. Dragons, however, are reptilian spirits of fire. A typical adversary in quest lore, the dragon is central to *The Hobbit*, but is hardly mentioned in *The Lord of the Rings*.

The Rings of Power are pivotal objects in Tolkien's works. Their purposes and powers are much like those of magic rings in mythology, enhanced by Tolkien's vivid and detailed imagination.

Weapons are traditionally given special significance. They have personalities attributed to them, they are named, and they are often credited with supernatural powers. Tolkien's treatment of the important weapons of Middle-earth parallels Celtic and Teutonic mythology.

Tolkien's description of barrows and their inhabitants contains so much of the mysterious and supernatural that it raises a number of questions. These can best be answered by examining the nature of barrows in reality and in myth.

13

Dragons

DRAGONS in Tolkien's works display the characteristics of typical dragons in European myth. The type of dragon that Tolkien portrayed was the cunning, long-lived, serpentine monster, "covetous, envious, venomous, spitting flame"[1] that seems synonymous with myth and fairy story.

In reality, dragons had a long history before they became the characteristic adversaries that we know. They probably had their origin in Asia, where they had a much different connotation than in Europe. Asian dragons were considered creatures of good omen, and were made up of a combination of features from a variety of symbolic or magic animals.

It has been suggested that the dragon figure was brought west by the Romans, who returned from conquests in the East bearing dragon banners as standards. These were in the form of windsleeves that stood out and writhed impressively overhead. The Europeans seem to have adapted the creatures portrayed on the banners to their own legends, adding their own symbolism and their own mythical features. Unlike the dragons of good omen in the Orient, or the serpents that brought healing or fertility in Mediterranean belief, the European dragon was evil, destructive, and without honor.

[1] Grimm, *Teutonic Mythology,* vol. II, p. 689.

European dragons are unique in having wings (often, and sometimes several pairs), a voracious appetite for human flesh, and firy breath. It has been hypothesized that these characteristics establish the dragon as symbolic of the funeral fires whose leaping flames consumed the dead.[2] It may have been with the same symbolic intent that dragons were portrayed as living under the earth, or, more to the point, in burial mounds, and as protecting the burial treasures of the dead.

The wings of European dragons had another significance. They carried the dragon through the air like shooting stars or comets, which were literally thought to be dragons. Belief in the malignant influence of celestial phenomena has persisted to the present day.

Fighting fire with fire, people in medieval times lit midsummer bonfires of bones and filth to drive off the dragons which they believed poisoned wells by mating over them. In Belgium, dragons were dispersed by lighting fires on Saint Peter's Day, the twenty-ninth of June.[3] These practices may be compared with the lighting of midsummer fires as a protection against Trolls.

Winged dragons were called drakes, while the wingless, such as Fafnir, were called worms, from the Scandinavian word *orm* ("snake").[4] Tolkien, however, used the terms interchangeably. He mentioned three types of dragons in Middle-earth: cold-drakes, fire-drakes, and were-worms. The first two types appeared in the histories, but the third type may have been only proverbial — the idea was likely to have been suggested by the story of Fafnir.

By the time the epics of Beowulf and Sigurd came to be

[2] Davidson, *Scandinavian Mythology*, pp. 119, 120.
[3] Frazer, *The Golden Bough*, pp. 720, 730.
[4] Grimm, vol. II, p. 688.

told, it was supposed that dragons had an all-too-human lust for gold. They found treasure in hoards and burials, made it their own and guarded it jealously, heaping up the gold to form their beds. From this habit, "worm-bed" became one of the standard kennings for gold.[5] The dragon's hoard is a favorite theme of Tolkien's. It is a subject of the humorous children's story, *Farmer Giles of Ham*, of the grim, moralistic poem "The Hoard" in *The Adventures of Tom Bombadil*, and of *The Hobbit*.

One of the most famous Teutonic stories about dragons, which inspired much in Tolkien's works, is the tale of Fafnir in the *Volsungsaga*. Fafnir was a were-worm, a human who had taken on the form of a dragon to hoard the gold for which he and his brother had murdered their father. At the instigation of Fafnir's brother, the hero Sigurd dug a pit on the dragon's path to water. From the pit he fatally stabbed the dragon from beneath with a reforged sword that had originally come from Odin.[6]

An even more elemental combat which demonstrates the dragon's fearful potential was the continuous rivalry between Thór and the Midgard-serpent. This huge serpent, Jörmungand, lay in the sea and encircled the world. It was prophesied that at Ragnarök Thór would slay the Midgards-orm, but would only stagger back nine paces before he died of its poison.[7] The same theme of the death of the hero by the poison of the dragon he has vanquished forms the climax of the story of Beowulf.

The combination of the themes of a magic ring and a dangerous serpent, themes central to *The Hobbit*, is found in the

[5] *Ibid.*
[6] Davidson, p. 100.
[7] Snorri Sturluson, *The Prose Edda*, p. 88.

story "Peredur Son of Evrawe" in *The Mabinogion*. One of
the adventures of Peredur (Percivale) was a combat with a
serpent that had desolated the land around him for seven miles
and that lay on a precious gold ring. Peredur slew the serpent
and took the ring.[8] The destruction wreaked by the serpent is
traditional, and appears in *The Hobbit* as the Desolation of
the Dragon, the wasteland around the Lonely Mountain.

A similar story about Peredur in the same source substituted
a treasure-yielding stone for the ring. Peredur encountered a
black, one-eyed man called the Black Oppressor, who had lost
one eye fighting the Black Serpent of the Carn. This serpent
lived in a carn called the Mound of Mourning. On its tail
was a stone of such virtue that if a man held it in one hand,
in the other he would have all the gold he desired. Peredur
killed the Black Oppressor and the serpent as well.[9]

Another theme concerning dragons, which is reflected in
the story of Smaug, is the dragon's association with water.
Fafnir lived by a river which contributed to his doom, the
Midgards-orm lived in the sea, as did the monster from which
Perseus rescued Andromeda, and many folk-tale dragons
guarded fountains. In this tradition, Smaug lived in the
Lonely Mountain, where the river that filled the Long Lake
had its source. Both river and dragon issued from the same
huge archway.

Wherever a dragon appears in Tolkien's works, it is wholly
within the tradition of European myth. Chrysophylax, the
dragon of Farmer Giles, and Smaug, in *The Hobbit*, were
tricky, covetous, honorless, and almost too clever for the
honest farmer and hobbit. Chrysophylax, Smaug, and the

---

[8] *The Mabinogion*, p. 198.
[9] *Ibid.*, p. 201.

dragon of "The Hoard" were underground treasure-hoarders somewhat like Fafnir, but more like the dragon of *Beowulf*, for in *Beowulf* the same purposeless covetousness is described at length.

Tolkien's dragons all also have the appearance of traditional mythic dragons: they are winged, four-legged fire-breathers. And Smaug, in Tolkien's own illustrations, has the curious upturned nose that is the consistent facial feature of dragons from the Viking northwest to the Javanese southeast, although it exists in no real reptiles except the crocodilians.

Curiously, the theme of the dragon with his hoard, a high point of *The Hobbit*, is completely absent in *The Lord of the Rings*. Once Tolkien left the adventure story for the ethical quest, the dragon became too stereotyped a symbol to use. In our culture, to "believe in dragons" is to be childishly credulous, and, in the face of that attitude, it is impossible even for Tolkien to imbue a dragon with the fundamental evil power of, for example, the Balrog. Furthermore, in the tradition of folk tales, dragons are doomed to be slain, and, no matter how awesomely they are depicted, it is inevitable that the hero will triumph over the beast. For *The Lord of the Rings*, Tolkien developed challenges and adversaries that are new to the reader and untried by centuries of literary combat, although they are themselves based on myth.

14

Rings of Power

As IN Tolkien's works, magic rings play an important part in myth and folk tale. The ancients held that even ordinary rings were powerful talismans, their gems having curative or protective powers, and rings were believed to have significant effects according to which finger they adorned. Scandinavian and Anglo-Saxon kings showed their generosity by distributing rings, arm-rings for the most part, to deserving followers, so that "ring-giver" became synonymous with good monarch. It is only a small step from these traditions to imagine the forces legendary magic rings were thought to wield.

The best-known rings in Teutonic mythology were those of Odin and Andvari. Like Tolkien's One Ring, both were powerful rings belonging to supernatural beings. The primary power of these Teutonic rings was that of increasing wealth. Odin's ring had only that power; perhaps it was a prototype wishing ring in accordance with Odin's postulated personification of Wish. The ring of Andvari had more of the malevolent nature of Sauron's ring. Indeed, Tolkien undoubtedly had Andvari's ring in mind when he composed *The Lord of the Rings*. Andvari's ring was accursed and brought corruption and tragedy to each of its bearers until it, like the One Ring, was consumed with its last owner in fire.

Odin's gold ring, made by Dwarves, was named Draupnir, ("Dripper"). It seems to have been an arm-ring rather than a finger-ring. Odin placed Draupnir on Balder's pyre, but Balder sent it back from Hel with Hermod. Thereafter, it dripped eight rings every ninth night, each of equal weight to Draupnir itself.[1]

The Dwarf Andvari's ring, like the One Ring, was a ring of doom. Its history is one of repeated covetousness and corruption, and both the moral and mythical elements of its story were adapted by Tolkien to the story of Sauron's Ring.

Like Draupnir, Andvari's ring had the power of increasing wealth. It was taken from Andvari by the god Loki to recompense Hreidmar for the accidental slaying of Hreidmar's son Otter. Because of the evil influence of the ring, the hoard did Hreidmar no good. His remaining sons, Fafnir and Regin, murdered him for the treasure. As discussed before, Fafnir transformed himself into a dragon, keeping all the treasure for himself.

Regin adopted Sigurd, son of the hero Sigmund, and persuaded him to kill Fafnir. Regin then plotted to kill Sigurd, but Sigurd was warned and killed Regin instead, taking the treasure and the ring.

The curse of the ring then fell upon Sigurd; he was killed by his brothers-in-law, Gunnar and Högni. Before his death he gave the ring to the valkyrie Byrnhild, who wore it on the funeral pyre when she slew herself at Sigurd's death. Gunnar and Högni hid the remaining gold from Andvari's hoard in the Rhine. It is because of this myth that gold was given the understated kenning "metal of strife."[2]

[1] Snorri Sturluson, *The Prose Edda*, p. 83.
[2] *Ibid.*, pp. 111–115.

The curious parallel between Andvari's ring and the One Ring is that neither corrupted simply through being precious and stimulating covetousness, but both were also inherently evil due to the spells cast by their first owners. Sigurd's story points to the hopelessness of even the greatest heroes in pitting themselves against fate. In *The Lord of the Rings*, where fate plays a more ambiguous part, the nature of the Ring underlines the magnitude of temptation with which the Ringbearer will continually be faced, and establishes the certainty that the Ring can never be used for good.

The theme of powerful rings is ubiquitous in Teutonic and Celtic mythology. The god Thór, like Odin, was associated with a powerful ring, probably representing the throwing-ring from which his hammer was suspended. Such a ring was kept in Thór's shrine, and at times was worn on the priest's arm. Most important, in view of Tolkien's works, Thór's ring was used to swear oaths upon, as the One Ring was sworn upon by Sméagol with an oath so binding that its breaking destroyed him.

In folk tales, magic rings were credited with diverse properties. In the Märchen, rings were described that permitted maidens to change into the shape of swans. In a French story a naked man was turned into a hunting wolf by the use of a ring.[3]

There are several accounts of magic rings in the Arthurian Cycle. In one, Dame Lionesse gave Sir Gareth a ring which disguised him at a tournament by changing the colors of his garments. More important, it also protected him from shedding blood.[4]

[3] Grimm, *Teutonic Mythology*, vol. I, p. 428; vol. III, p. 1096.
[4] Malory, *Le Morte Darthur*, vol. I, p. 284.

In "The Lady of the Fountain" in *The Mabinogion*, Owain son of Urien was trapped between the inner gate and the portcullis of an enemy's castle. Luned (Lunette), handmaiden to the countess of the castle, rescued him. She gave him a ring and told him to put it on his finger with the stone to the inside of his hand. As long as he closed his hand, concealing the stone, he was himself invisible. He did so, and escaped when the people of the castle saw no one inside and opened the inner gate.[5] Welsh legend has it that this ring, as one of the thirteen rarities of kingly regalia, was imprisoned with Merlin in a glass castle on Bardsley Island.[6]

The story of Owain's ring exemplifies the comment by Grimm that finger-rings that lend victory or invisibility do so by virtue of the stones set in them.[7] In contrast, all the rings of power of *The Lord of the Rings* except the One Ring were marked by their special stones, yet only the One Ring was specifically mentioned as lending invisibility.

The stones of the three Elven Rings had the colors of the unearthly elements water, fire, and air. Each Ring was named for one of these elements and each apparently gave power over that element to the wearer. The effects of Elrond's blue Ring of Air are uncertain, but Galadriel's clear Ring of Water may have been related to the magic of her fountain and her land bordered by rivers. There is no question of the powers lent by Gandalf's Ring of Flame, as effective in arranging birthday-party fireworks as in combatting the Balrog.

The Ring's colors may have another significance older than the theory of the elements. According to Robert Graves, the recurring color sequence, white, red, and blue, symbolized the

[5] *The Mabinogion*, p. 159.
[6] *Ibid.*, p. 372.
[7] Grimm, vol. II, p. 1221.

lunar-vegetation-mother goddess as new, full, and old moon, and as maiden, bride, and crone.[8]

The One Ring of Tolkien's works has a dual nature. In *The Hobbit* it is an innocent talisman, magic, but in no way foreshadowing its ominous future. Like Owain's ring, it is a magic ornament that gives the hero additional aid and helps him to appreciate his own potential, not least by keeping him alive long enough to develop his heroism.

In *The Lord of the Rings*, the Ring has a very different significance. It represents the enslaving potential of precious possessions and of unlimited power, an evil that is inherent in the Ring but is realized only to the degree that weakness or evil already exists in the possessor. Like Andvari's "metal of strife," Sauron's gold carries a curse that finally touches even the free-handed, lighthearted Bilbo and lays an almost unbearable burden on his heir. It is no longer just a fairy-tale ring, a wish-ring, but the repository of the destructive force of an evil power and intelligence. The irony is that if it were not also a wish-ring, if it were not precious and did not confer power, it would not have been evil and could not have enslaved anyone.

[8] Graves, *The White Goddess*, p. 71.

15

Weapons

THE IMPORTANT WEAPONS in Tolkien's works are wholly in the traditions of myth. They are counted highly valuable, "worth many a mortal man, even the mightiest."[1] They are given awesome and descriptive names and their origins are mysterious: they are made by Elves or Dwarves or wrought in ancient Westernesse. They have colorful, supernatural histories and mysterious qualities, many of which parallel actual myths. They are worthy of their wielders, enhancing their legendary quality of heroism.

Historically, good personal weapons were rare until the late Middle Ages, and were primarily carried by nobles. Because of their rarity and their value in war, certain weapons were credited with a supernatural history and magic powers. Swords made of the revolutionary metal, iron, were automatically considered charmed.[2]

Many weapons in myth were also supposed to have been made by supernatural beings. Thór's hammer and Odin's spear were attributed to the smithcraft of Dwarves. Several Teutonic heroes, including Beowulf, carried swords that were

[1] Tolkien, *The Two Towers*, p. 118.
[2] *The Elder Edda*, p. 25.

believed to have been forged by Völund (Weyland) the Smith, known as the Lord of the Elves.[3]

In Tolkien's works, the first theme of a supernatural weapon is that of a magic sword that changes the character of its possessor. This theme is central to both *The Hobbit* and *Farmer Giles of Ham*.

In *Farmer Giles*, the farmer drove off a giant and was awarded an old sword by the king. Later, when a dragon menaced the farmer's neighborhood, it was discovered that the weapon was the famed, ancient Caudimorax ("Tailbiter"). The knowledge that he possessed a famous sword (as well as the effect of a certain amount of ale) gave Giles the courage to face the cunning dragon.

In *The Hobbit*, Bilbo was similarly encouraged when he discovered that his small sword Sting was an Elven-blade from Gondolin. It gave him confidence in the Goblin-holes and the courage to attack the giant spiders of Mirkwood.

Both Bilbo's sword Sting and Farmer Giles' sword Tailbiter were magic in that they gave warning of approaching danger. Ancient Elven-swords, including Sting, Gandalf's sword Glamdring, and Thorin's blade Orcrist, glowed with a mysterious blue light when Orcs were nearby. By the intensity of the glow, the number and distance of the enemy could be guessed. Farmer Giles' sword gave warning in that if a dragon were within five miles, the sword would leap from its sheath.

Accounts of glowing swords and weapons that warn of the coming of an enemy are widespread in myth. When the Scandinavian gods entertained Aegir, Odin's hall was entirely

[3] *Ibid.*, p. 29.

illuminated with bright swords.[4] According to Malory, King Arthur's sword Excalibur gave off a light like thirty torches.[5] In the Cuchulain Cycle, Dubthach of Ulster had a spear called Celthair's Luin which was used in the battle of Magh Tuireadh. When battle was near, it would flame up and had to be quenched in a vessel, otherwise its battle fury would grow until it pierced whoever held it.[6] Another alarm-giving piece of battle gear in the Cuchulain Cycle was a shield called the Ochain ("the Moaning One"), which belonged to Conchubar, Cuchulain's uncle. It would moan whenever Conchubar was in danger, and all the shields of Ulster would moan in answer.[7]

Another supernatural quality is seen in two weapons in *The Lord of the Rings* that magically burned away after they had interacted between the mortal world and the Wraith world. One was the Morgul knife with which the Black Rider stabbed Frodo on Weathertop; the other was the barrow-blade with which Meriadoc stabbed the Black Captain of the Nazgûl. A similar event occurred when Beowulf found a magic sword in Grendel's underwater den and used it to cut off the dead Grendel's head. The sword blade dissolved in Grendel's hot blood, leaving only the golden, rune-covered hilt.[8]

The value of good weapons was so great in ancient times that many weapons were given names and titles and held to have individual identities. This was particularly true in the Scandinavian countries. The Anglo-Saxons, who had a rich variety of expressive kennings for weapons, seldom gave them individual names. Beowulf's sword Nagling and Unferd's sword Hrunting in *Beowulf* may be taken as exceptions; however, *Beowulf* is an account of events in Scandinavia.

[4] Snorri Sturluson, *The Prose Edda*, p. 97.
[5] Malory, *Le Morte Darthur*, vol. I, p. 23.
[6] Gregory, *Cuchulain of Muirthemne*, p. 87.
[7] *Ibid.*, p. 50.
[8] *Beowulf*, 1557–1698.

Throughout Tolkien's works all the most important weapons have names. Glamdring, Orcrist, and Sting have been mentioned. In Rohan, the important weapons were Éomer's sword Guthwine and Théoden's sword Herugrim. Guthwine ("Battle-friend") is not a name but is a standard Old English kenning for any sword. Herugrim means "Angry in Battle." Even the forces of Mordor had a named weapon. The battering ram that broke the gates of Minas Tirith was named Grond after Morgoth's Mace, the Hammer of the Underworld.

The most valued weapon was Aragorn's sword, Andúril. It was forged by Telchar "in the deeps of time" which suggests that it came with Elendil from Númenor. Its original name was Narsil ("Red and White Flame") because it shone red in the sunlight and cold under the moon. It broke under Elendil's body when he was slain by Sauron, but Elendil's son Isildur used the hilt-half to cut away Sauron's Ring. Narsil became an heirloom of Isildur's house and was known as the Sword That Was Broken. Aragorn carried it until he was chosen to the Fellowship of the Ring. Then, as had been prophesied, the sword was reforged and Aragorn renamed it Andúril, Flame of the West.

Not only was Andúril highly valued, but its sheath, given to Aragorn by Galadriel, had special powers. This jeweled sheath had such a virtue that no sword drawn from it would be stained or broken, even in defeat. This quality recalls the scabbard of Excalibur, which was even more valuable than the sword. While King Arthur wore the scabbard he could lose no blood, no matter how sorely he was wounded.[9]

The theme of broken and reforged swords appears both in the Arthurian Cycle and in the *Volsungsaga*. Both of these

9 Malory, vol. I, p. 57.

mythic cycles seem to have influenced Tolkien's use of the device. In the Arthurian Grail Romances there are swords that broke upon the death of their owners and could only be restored through the virtue of their successors. The reforging of the sword was often a condition of the successor's achieving a quest.[10] This is exactly the situation outlined in *The Lord of the Rings*.

Several accounts of broken swords appear in Malory's *Le Morte Darthur*. Two important examples are found in the adventure of the Holy Grail. In that account there was a magic sword which had been devised by King Solomon from King David's sword. Its hilts were inlaid with jewels and magic bones, and its sheath was inlaid with wood of the tree of life. The sword and the ship in which it lay were made at King Solomon's command for Sir Galahad, the last of King Solomon's lineage, of whom Solomon had heard by prophecy. No one but Sir Galahad could draw that sword without suffering wounds or death. The first stroke dealt by the sword laid two lands waste. Later the sword broke in the hand of Nacien when he needed it most, but the sword became whole at the touch of Nacien's brother-in-law, King Mordrains. Later, when King Pelles, Sir Galahad's grandfather, drew the sword, he received supernatural wounds that would not heal. Thus he was called the Maimed King until Sir Galahad healed him after fulfilling the quest of the Grail.

During the same adventure, King Pelles' son brought out the broken sword that had wounded Joseph, son of Joseph of Arimathea. Only Sir Galahad had the virtue to make the sword whole at his touch. That evening the sword rose up and put out a fierce heat, introducing a miraculous event.[11]

[10] Loomis, *Celtic Myth and Arthurian Romance*, p. 244.
[11] Malory, vol. II, Book 17, Chs. 3–6, 19, 21.

Two themes essential to the Arthurian Cycle are also central to the *Volsungsaga*. These are the theme of the sword that is broken and reforged, and that of the embedded sword that only one person can withdraw.

In the *Volsungsaga*, the god Odin, protector and forefather of Sigmund's line, embedded the sword Gram up to the hilt in the tree that formed the central pillar of Sigmund's family hall. Only Sigmund could draw it out, and by doing so he won Odin's favor. He fought for Odin for many years until the god determined that it was time for Sigmund to join his ancestors in the otherworld. Odin met Sigmund in the midst of a battle and broke Sigmund's sword so that he was overcome in the fighting. In obedience to Sigmund's dying wish, the fragments of his sword, like those of Elendil's sword Narsil, were preserved. The sword Gram was reforged by Regin for Sigmund's son Sigurd to use in killing Regin's brother, Fafnir the dragon.[12]

[12] Snorri Sturluson, *The Prose Edda*, pp. 111–112.

16

Barrows

TOLKIEN gives so much significance to barrows that it might be well to present some perspective on barrows in reality and in myth. To see the little mounds on the downs around Stonehenge, placidly grazed by uncaring cattle, may be to wonder where the mystery lies. But there are bigger barrows in more desolate settings, and they are far from disappointing.

Archaeologically speaking, barrows or tumuli are large artificial mounds used for burials in western Europe. It is a type of burial that originated in the Neolithic Period and continued to be used through the Viking age. The word barrow comes from the Old English word *beorg*, related to *berg* ("mountain").

Barrows usually consist of a stone box or chamber, sometimes only loosely constructed of megaliths, which contain the body and the possessions of the deceased. The whole chamber would be covered over with a mound, usually of earth, but sometimes entirely of local stone. The mounds are either oval or circular and are often ringed with stones and are sometimes associated with standing stones placed singly or in alignments. One such is Silbury Hill in England, standing by the large, ruined, Stonehenge-like circle of Avebury. Silbury Hill is the largest barrow in Europe — five acres in area.

Barrows often stood in high places as landmarks and sometimes formed a line beside ancient trails. For example, in Old
Uppsala, Sweden, there is a striking alignment of about half
a dozen fifth-to-sixth-century barrows which are visible from
a distance across the comparatively flat land. At the head of
the row of barrows is a larger mound where the council met.
This alignment is just opposite the site of an important pagan
temple where the Old Uppsala Church now stands.

In mythic tradition the simple existence of a barrow was
thought to be enough to cause supernatural events in the
vicinity. Because of their antiquity, their connection with
forgotten dead, and their dominance of the landscape, barrows
were thought to be surrounded with an aura of enchantment.

A typical example of the sort of event held to take place
at barrows occurs in "Pwyll Prince of Dyvved" in *The
Mabinogion*. An episode is centered around a mound called
Gorsedd Arberth which was so enchanted that anyone who
sat on it would either receive wounds or see a wonder. Pwyll
dared the adventure and repeatedly saw from the barrow a
lady dressed in gold riding a large white horse that could not
be overtaken. She was Rhiannon, whom Pwyll later married.[1]

A more famous medieval tale, the poem *Sir Gawain and the
Green Knight*, makes a barrow the site of the knight's trial of
chivalry. The barrow is inconsistently described as a fairy
place, fit for Satan's devotion, but called the Green Chapel.
There Sir Gawain finally confronts the Green Knight and is
tested in honor and bravery.

In Irish mythology, the building of barrows was ascribed
to the Sidhe, the Elves. It was believed that mortals could
reach immortal faerie lands through the barrows' mouth. Such

[1] *The Mabinogion*, p. 18.

barrows were the "hollow hills" of legend where the dead or the Sidhe could be heard inside. However, natural hills and mountains also were thought to house the living dead.

Because of the tenuousness of the barrier between the real world and the otherworld that was thought to exist at barrows, it was an ancient practice to go to the burial mounds to communicate with the dead. Sometimes councils were held on the mounds, as at Uppsala, where it was hoped that the dead king's presence might lend wisdom. Kings and seers were reputed to have sat on burial mounds to make a claim to the title of the former king or to gain inspiration. In doing so they sometimes apparently encountered supernatural powers or underwent strange experiences. It seems to have been customary in this way to seek inspiration from the king underground.[2]

An important Scandinavian myth described a typical example of seeking advice from the dead in a barrow. When the god Balder had the dreams that portended his death and the eventual Twilight of the Gods, Odin went to the barrow of a seeress and conjured her with runes to come out and foretell the future.[3]

Sometimes barrows were reputed to hold ancient weapons that had supernatural qualities. There is a tradition that such a sword was used at the birth of King Olaf the Holy of Norway. Olaf's birth was said to have proved so difficult that magic had to be used. At last, when the sword of a previous King Olaf, symbolizing the continuation of the royal line, had been brought from the barrow of the old king and the sword-belt laid around the mother, the child was safely

2 Davidson, *Scandinavian Mythology*, p. 87.
3 *The Elder Edda*, p. 116.

delivered. It was said that the symbolic sword was kept by the mother and handed down to the young king, who was considered a reincarnation of his predecessor.[4]

A more gruesome account of the seeking of a barrow sword is the theme of "Waking of Angantyr" in the *Elder Edda*. The story describes Hervor, the daughter of Angantyr the berserk, going to the grave mounds when they were gaping open and wreathed with supernatural flame. There she confronted her dead father, requesting his sword. The sword, Tyrfing, with poisoned edges, had been forged by the Dwarf Dvalin. Angantyr repeatedly warned Hervor that the sword would destroy all her kindred, but at last he gave it to her for her courage in facing the grave-fire.[5]

Tolkien's development of the theme of swords won from a barrow is in the tradition of myth. The hobbits' barrow-blades, like Olaf's and Angantyr's, had supernatural powers which seemed to come less from association with the dead than with their makers and first owners. The hobbits' swords had been made by the Dúnedain at the time of the wars with the Witch-king. The swords were furnished with spells against the Witch-king and his servants, which took immediate effect when Meriadoc wounded the Witch-king himself, who had become the Black Captain of the Nazgûl.

Throughout *The Lord of the Rings* Tolkien developed both the burial tradition and the mythic tradition of barrows in accordance with actual usage. He gave barrows a long history in Middle-earth comparable to the antiquity of the actual barrow-building tradition. In Middle-earth, barrows were first raised by the forefathers of the Edain and later by

[4] Davidson, p. 87.
[5] *The Elder Edda*, pp. 101–105.

two branches of their descendants, the northern Dúnedain and the Rohirrim. In the First Age, the ancestors of the Edain raised barrows in the place later called the Barrow Downs, Tyrn Gorthad. When their descendants, the Dúnedain, returned from Númenor to Middle-earth, they revered the ancient burial places and continued to use them for the burial of their kings and nobles.

After the defeat of Arnor, the barrows became inhabited by barrow-wights, undefined evil creatures from the Witch-king's realm in Angmar. It was suggested that the barrow in which Frodo and his companions were imprisoned by a barrow-wight was that of the last prince of Cardolan, a subdivision of Arnor. "Wight" simply means a being, a creature, or a thing (as seen in the cognate "whit"), and was used to refer to both humans and animals. In Old Norse, however, the word suggested a demonic, supernatural creature, a usage comparable to Tolkien's.[6]

The tradition of evil spirits in burial places is of great antiquity. Guardian spirits were supposed to ensure that the rituals and laws concerning the dead were obeyed. The spirits of the dead themselves were thought to return to haunt those who had not observed proper funeral traditions.

Thus, the account of Frodo's adventure on the Barrow Downs is in accordance with mythic tradition. The adventure not only concerned the spell-singing evil wight, but the barrow's dead as well. The hobbits were threatened by the Dead Hand, and also dreamed that they were the barrow's dead, slain by the Witch-king's forces from Carn Dûm in a battle that took place an age of the world ago. They woke to find themselves dressed in the funeral robes and gold common to that distant time.

[6] Grimm, *Teutonic Mythology*, vol. II, p. 440.

The supernatural aura of the barrows at the Barrow Downs, the deadly spirits that inhabited them, and the grotesque events that occurred in and near them are based on extensive mythic traditions. Barrows were held by the ancients to house vengeful dead plotting to destroy the living, wise dead able to confer counsel, and heirlooms and weapons with awesome powers.

In contrast to the northern barrows, the burial mounds in Rohan were not viewed with horror. Unlike the northern mounds, those in Rohan were comparatively new, stood in a well-frequented location, and housed the remains of well-known kings. The barrow-ground of Rohan was divided by family line, so the nine mounds on the left as seen going toward Edoras held the kings from Eorl to Helm. The eight on the right-hand side of the road were the tombs of the kings from Helm's sister-son Fréalaf Hildeson to Théoden. A new line started with Théoden's sister-son Éomer.

The account of Théoden's burial is an accurate depiction of tumulus burial. The king was laid in a house of stone with his arms and treasure, and a high mound covered with turves was built over him. Except for the absence of a pyre, it is like the burial of Beowulf, another king who died in victorious battle which he undertook although aged. For both kings a song of mourning was sung, for each, horsemen rode around the completed mounds singing the king's praise.[7]

[7] *Beowulf*, 3150–3174.

GLOSSARY

BIBLIOGRAPHY

INDEX

GLOSSARY

THIS SECTION glosses many of the Old English and other obscure words and names used in Tolkien's works. In this glossary, the word or name is followed by the abbreviation of the language that is the source of the word. If the source word had a different spelling from that used by Tolkien, the original spelling is given in italics. The translation of the source word is given in quotation marks. The context of the word in Tolkien's works is given in parentheses.

The primary sources for this glossary were Bosworth and Toller's *Anglo-Saxon Dictionary*, *The Oxford English Dictionary* in 12 volumes, first published in 1933, and Tolkien's "Guide to the Names in *The Lord of the Rings*," published in *A Tolkien Compass*, edited by Lobdell.

KEY TO ABBREVIATIONS

arch.	archaic English		lish used since c1475)
Celt.	Celtic	obs.	obsolete English
dial.	dialect of English	OE	Old English (the English
Dan.	Danish		language c450–c1150)
Goth.	Gothic	OHG	Old High German (High
Icel.	Icelandic		German used before
L	Latin		c1100)
ME	Middle English (the English language c1150–c1475)	ON	Old Norse
		Scand.	Scandinavian
		Scot.	Scottish
mod.	Modern English (Eng-	Swed.	Swedish

Afterlithe. OE *aefter-lith* "July" (the name for July in the Shire)

Afteryule. OE *aefter-geóla* "January" (the hobbits' name for January)

Aldor. OE "an elder, chief" (a king of Rohan who lived to a great age)

Anborn. OE *án-boren* "only-born, "only-begotten" (a Ranger of Ithilien)

Andwise Roper. OE *and-wís* "expert, skillful" (a hobbit)

Anson Roper. OE *án, sunu* "only son" (a hobbit, an only son)

Arkenstone. OE *eorcan-stán* "genuine, holy stone" (a large, glowing crystal jewel, the heart of the Lonely Mountain)

Arod. OE "quick, swift, ready" (the horse Legolas and Gimli rode in Rohan)

Astron. OE *Easter-monath* "April" (the name for April in the Shire)

Athelas. OE *athel* "noble" with plural suffix (Aragorn's healing herb)

Baldor. OE "more bold, courageous, honorable, hence a prince, ruler" (son of a king of Rohan, lost on the Paths of the Dead)

Bard. OE hypothesized original form of the OE word *beard* "beard"; Celt. "poet" (man of Lake-town who killed Smaug the Dragon)

Béma. OE *bema* "trumpet" (the name in Rohan for Oromë, the Huntsman of the Valar)

Beorn. OE "man, hero"; Dan. Swed. Icel. *bjorn* "bear" (a man of Wilderland who could change into a bear)

Beren. OE "like a bear, ursine" (Elf-friend who recovered the Silmaril from Morgoth)

Bilbo. arch. a slender sword or rapier known for its temper, from Bilbao, Spain, famous for its steel (a hobbit who had a magic sword)

Blooting, Blotmath. OE *blotmonath* "November, month of heathen sacrifice" (Blooting was the name in Bree for November which the Shirefolk called Blotmath)

Brand. OE "firebrand, torch" (a king of Dale descended from
Bard)

Bree. arch. "a bank, hill" (a town on a hill east of the Shire)

Brego. OE "leader, ruler, prince, king." Brego was the name of
the Teutonic god of poetic eloquence, also named Bragi,
whence our word "brag" (a king of Rohan)

Breredon. ME *brere*, OE *dún* "briar hill" (a village in the Shire)

Brock. OE *broc* "badger"

Brytta. OE "bestower, dispenser, distributor, hence a prince,
lord" (a very open-handed king of Rohan)

Budgeford. Tolkien's variation on "bulge, ford" (a ford and a
village in the Shire, the folkland of the bulgy Bolgers)

Carl. ME, OE "churl" from Scand. *karl* "man" (the name of some
hobbits)

Carrock. North. dial. "stone, rock" from OE *carr* "stone, rock"
and OE *rocc* "rock"; compare Scot. *cairn* (a stone island in
the Upper Anduin River)

Ceorl. OE "a freeman of the lowest class, churl, husbandman"
(a rider of Rohan)

Chithing. OE *cith* "a sprout" (the name for April in Bree)

Combe. Celt. "narrow valley or deep hollow" (a village in Bree-
land. Coomb, as in Deeping Coomb, the valley below Hornburg, has the same meaning)

Dain. Icel. *Dáinn* "corpse" (the name of two kings of the
Dwarves)

Déagol. OE "secret, unknown" (Gollum's best friend, finder of
the One Ring)

Déor. OE "deer, wild animal, brave or bold as a wild beast" (a
king of Rohan)

Deorwine. OE "deer friend, friend of animals" (a rider of Rohan)

Derndingle. OE *dern*, ME *dingle* "secret dell" (the hollow where
Entmoots were held)

Dernhelm. OE "secret helmet, helmet of secrecy" (the name Eowyn took when she rode, disguised in armor, to Gondor)

Dior. OE *diore* "dear, precious, glorious, magnificent"; the less appropriate OE *dior* means "dire, a beast" (the son of Lúthien and Beren, father of Elwing)

Dunharg, Dunharrow. OE *dún hearg* "hill temple" (a secret temple in Rohan built by forgotten peoples, probably the ancestors of the Dead)

Dúnhere. OE "hill warrior" (a rider of Rohan)

Dunland, Dunlending. OE *dún-land* "hill-land, down-land," in contrast to OE *feld-land* "plain-land, level-land"; Tolkien makes a scholarly pun when he derives Dunland from OE *dunn* "dark, brown" because of the swarthy coloring of the Dunlendings (lands and their wild inhabitants west of Rohan)

Durin. Icel. *Durinn,* one of two mysterious princes who formed new Dwarves out of earth (the longfather of the Dwarves)

Dwalin. Icel. *Dvalinn* "one lying in a trance" (a Dwarf of Thorin's company)

Dwaling. OE *dwelian* "to go astray, to wander" (a village in the Shire, so called because it is so far afield as to be off the map, at the end of a winding road)

Dwerrowdelf. Tolkien's construction for "Dwarf-delving." Dwerrow is an artificial word showing how OE *dweorg* "dwarf" might have evolved to parallel *beorg* "barrow" (the translation of Phurunargian, Westron for Khazad-dûm, Moria)

Dwimmerlaik. ME *dweomerlaik* "legerdemain" OE *dwimor* "illusion"; ME *laik* "play" (Eowyn's belittling word for the Black Captain of the Nazgûl)

Dwimorberg. OE "mountain of phantoms" (the mountain under which lay the Paths of the Dead)

Dwimordene. OE "valley of illusion"; OE *dwimor* "illusion, delusion, phantom, apparition" (the Rohirrim's name for Lórien)

Eärendil. OE *eorendil* "light, the first dawn." The OE word is derived from the name of the star Earendel or Orentil which in turn was named for the hero from which it was created. The name is also Quenya: "sea-lover, lover of the middle of the sea" (a hero and the Morning Star which he became)

Eastemnet. OE "east plain" (the lands of Rohan east of the Entwash)

Easterlings. dial. "natives of the east" (allies of Sauron from the east)

Eastfold. OE "east earth" (an eastern part of Rohan)

Edoras. OE "dwellings, places enclosed by a barrier" ("the Courts," the king's city in Rohan)

Elfhelm. OE "elf helmet" (a rider of Rohan)

Elfhild. OE "elf battle" (Théoden's wife. See the note on Hild.)

Elfstan Fairbairn. arch. "elf-stone fair-child" (a hobbit, surnamed for the fair hair and faces common in the decendants of Samwise and Rose, and named for Aragorn Elessar "Elf-stone.") *Elfstone* is the name once given to old stone arrowheads believed to have been shot at cattle by fairies, causing disease. Elphinstone and Elbenstein are names of noble families.

Elfwine. OE "Elf-friend" (a king of Rohan, son of Eomer)

Elvet Isle. arch. "a tiny elf" (an island in the Withywindle where a swan lived. This is a pun on the OE *elf* "elf" and OE *aelfet* "swan," probably related words)

Ent. OE "giant"; compare *eten, eoten* "giant" (a benevolent tree-giant of Fangorn Forest)

Éomer. OE. This name appears in *Beowulf* (a hero and king of Rohan)

Éomund. OE "horse hand" *eh* "a warhorse," *mund* "hand" (a rider of Rohan)

Éored. OE "cavalry" (cavalry unit of Rohan)

Eorl. OE "a nobleman of high rank, an earl" (the first king of Rohan)

Eorlingas. OE "descendants of Eorl" (another name for the Rohirrim)

Éothain. OE "horse thane" *eh* "a warhorse," *thegn* "thane, a member of any of several classes between earls and freemen" (a rider of Rohan)

Éothéod. OE "horse folk" (the ancestors of the Rohirrim and their land in the north)

Éowyn. OE "horsewoman, one who delights in horses"? *eh* "a warhorse," *wyn* an epithet of persons, also meaning "delight, pleasure" (renowned woman of Rohan)

Erkenbrand. OE "chief? torch" *erk* "chief," *brand* "firebrand, torch" (a rider of Rohan)

Ettendales, Ettenmoors. OE "giant-valleys, giant-moors"; OE *eten* "a giant"; compare OE *ent* and *eóten*. Grendel in *Beowulf* was an *eóten; eóten* also means Jutlander, as *Hune*, another word for giant, also means Hun. Dale is from OE *dael* "broad valley," moor from OE *mor* "peaty wasteland" (Troll-lands north of Rivendell)

Fallohides. mod. *fallow, hide* "pale-yellow pelt" (the most adventurous tribe of hobbits, so called for their fair hair)

Farthing. mod. "a fourth part" (any one of the four main divisions of the Shire)

Fastitocalon. OE "great whale" (a "turtle-fish" which could be mistaken for an island in the poem "Fastitocalon" in *The Adventures of Tom Bombadil*)

Fastred. OE "firm counsel" (a king of Rohan's son)

Felaróf. OE "very valiant, strong" (the horse of Eorl, king of Rohan)

Fengel. OE "prince" (a king of Rohan)

Ferdibrand Took. OE *ferd, brand* "army torch" (a hobbit)

Firienfeld, Firienwood. OE *firgen, feld, wudu* "mountain field, mountain wood" (the field of Dunharrow and a forest at the foot of the White Mountains)

Flet. OE "floor, dwelling" (a platform in a tree used in Lórien either as the floor of a dwelling or as a dwelling in itself)

Folca. OE *folc* "folk, people" (a king of Rohan)

Folcred. OE "counselor of the people" (a king of Rohan's son, brother of Fastred)

Folcwine. OE "friend of the people" (a king of Rohan, son of King Folca, father of Folcred and Fastred)

Folde. OE *fold* "the earth" (a part of Rohan)

Forelithe. OE *lith* "months of June and July" (the hobbits' name for June)

Foreyule. OE *geóla* "December" (the hobbits' name for December)

Forn. Scand. "ancient, sorcery" (the Dwarvish name for Bombadil)

Fram. OE "firm, valiant, stout" (a lord of Eothéod)

Fréa. OE "lord, master" (a king of Rohan)

Fréaláf. OE "survivor of lords" (a king of Rohan, so named because as Helm's nephew he became his heir when Helm and his sons died during the Long Winter)

Fréawine. OE "dear or beloved lord" (a king of Rohan, son of Fréa)

Freca. OE "a bold man, warrior, hero" from *frec* "greedy, audacious" (a greedy, proud man of Rohan who set himself up as Helm's rival)

Fredigar Bolger. OE *ferd, gar* "army spear" (a hobbit, friend of Frodo)

Frery. OE *freorig* "freezing, cold" (the name in Bree for January)

Frodo. OE *fród* "wise, prudent, sage"; *freoda* "protector, defender"; *freodo* "peace, security"; the name Froda appears in *Beowulf* (a hobbit, the Ring-bearer)

Frumgar. OE "first spear, swift spear"; *frum* "original, primitive, first," or, less commonly "vigorous, prompt, swift" (first lord of Eothéod)

Fundin. Icel. "found one" (a Dwarf, father of Balin and Dwalin)

Galdor. OE "an incantation, enchantment, magic"; Sindarin "green land" (an Elf of the Grey Havens)

Gálmód. OE "light, wanton mood" (father of Grima Worm-tongue)

Gamling. OE "old one"; *gamol* "old, aged" (an old man of Rohan)

Gandalf. Icel. *Ganndálf* "sorcerer-elf" (a wizard)

Garulf. OE "spear wolf"? *gar, wulf* "wolf" (a rider of Rohan)

Gimli. Icel. "lee of flame, the highest heaven" (a Dwarf, one of the Company of the Ring)

Gladden River, Gladden Fields. ME *gladdon* "sword lily, iris" from L *gladius* "sword"; possibly a punning reference to the fact that the area not only bore fields of flag lilies, but was also the site of two famous battles (a river tributary to the Anduin and fields near it)

Gléowine. OE "friend of minstrels" (Théoden's minstrel)

Goldwine. OE "gold friend" (a king of Rohan)

Goldfimbul. Icel. *fimbul* "unearthly" (a goblin chief, unwitting originator of the sport named for him when he was killed with a club that knocked his head off and down a rabbit hole)

Gram, Mount Gram. OE "furious, fierce, wroth, angry" (a king of Rohan and one of the Misty Mountains)

Grima Wormtongue. OE *grim* "grim, fierce, cruel, a mask, a specter"; *grimena* "a caterpillar" (Théoden's traitorous counselor)

Grimbeorn. OE "grim man" (son of Beorn)

Grimbold of Grimslade. OE "grim-house of grim-valley" (a rider of Rohan)

Grindwall. Orkney and Shetland dial. from ON *grind* "a barred gate"; mod. *wall* (a village in Buckland)

Grond. obs. "grind" (the battering-ram used against Minas Tirith, and Morgoth's Mace, for which it was named)

Guthláf. OE "survivor of battle" (Théoden's standard-bearer who died in the battle of Pelennor Field)

Gúthwine. OE "battle-friend" a common OE kenning for swords (Eomer's sword)

Haleth. OE "more hale" *hál, eth* "more easily" (Helm's son)

Halfast. OE "secure in a dwelling" *heall* "hall" or *halh* "nook, secret place"; *fast* "snug, secure" (a hobbit)

Halfred. OE "half counseled" (the name of several hobbits)

Halimath. OE *halig-monath* "September, holy-month, month of heathen sacrifice" (the name of September in the Shire)

Halifirien. OE *halig, firgen* "holy mountain" (a beacon-hill in Firienwood)

Háma. OE "a coat of mail" (the name of Helm's youngest son and of Théoden's doorward)

Hamfast. OE *hám, fast* "stay-at-home" (the name of several hobbits)

Hamson. OE *hám, sunu* "home son" (a hobbit)

Harding. OE *hearding* "a brave man, warrior, hero" (a rider of Rohan)

Harfoots. dial. "hair feet" (the most representative type of hobbit)

Hasufel. OE "grey coat" *hasu* "grey, tawny, ash-colored" (Aragorn's horse in Rohan)

Haysend. dial. "hedge's end" from ME *haie* (a village in Buckland at the end of the High Hay)

Helm. OE "helmet" (a king of Rohan)

Herefara. OE "war farer" (a rider of Rohan)

Herubrand. OE "war torch" (a rider of Rohan)

Herugrim. OE "fierce in war" (Théoden's sword)

Hild. OE "battle"; this is probably considered an appropriate name for a woman because it was the name of a Valkyrie (Helm's sister)

Hildibrand Took. OE "battle torch" (a hobbit)

Hildifons Took. "battle fool"? OE *hild*, obs. *fon* "fool" (a hobbit)

Hildigard Took. OE "battle yard" (a hobbit)
Hildigrim Took. OE "grim in battle" (a hobbit)
Holbytla. OE "hole builder" (OE version of the word "hobbit" used to translate the Rohirrim's word *kud-dukkan*)
Holdwine. OE "true friend" (the name Eomer gave Meriadoc)
Holfast Gardner. OE "snug in hole" (a hobbit)
Holman. OE "hole man" (the name of several hobbits)
Horn. OE "horn" (a rider of Rohan)
Hornburg. OE "horn fortress" (the fortress in Rohan defending Helm's Deep)

Incánus. L "quite grey" (the name given Gandalf in the south)
Irensaga. OE "iron saw" (a sawtoothed mountain near Dunharrow)
Isembard Took. OE *isen, bard* "iron beard" (a hobbit)
Isembold Took. OE *isen, bold* "iron house" (a hobbit)
Isen River. OE "iron" (a river forming the western boundary of Rohan)
Isengar Took. OE "iron spear" (a hobbit)
Isengard. OE "iron yard" *geard* enclosure. Tolkien uses *gard* to combine the meanings of Old French *garde* "guard" and OE *geard* "yard" to describe a place which is both an enclosure and a fortress (Saruman's fortress)
Isengrim. OE "iron-mask" (the name of three Thains of the Took family)

Láthspell. OE "evil news." Compare *loathe* with OE *godspell* "good news" which provided the ME word *gospel* (the name Wormtongue called Gandalf)
Léod. OE "man, one of a people or country" (a lord of Eothéod, father of Eorl)
Léofa. OE *leof* "loved, dear" (the name given to Brytta, a very generous king of Rohan)
Lithe. OE *lith* "the months of June and July" (the name in the

Shire for the intercalary days between June and July, and the
name in Bree for June)

Long Cleeve. ME "long cliff" (a place in the Shire)

Marish. dial. "marsh" (a marshy part of the Shire near the Brandywine River)

Mark. OE *mearc* "territory within a boundary" (Rohan)

Mathom. OE *mathum* "a precious or valuable thing, often a gift"
(in the Shire, a gift for which there is little use but which one
does not want to discard)

Mearas. OE "horses" (the horses of the kings of Rohan)

Mede. OE *med* "middle" (the name in Bree for July)

Meduseld. OE "mead-hall." A standard OE word for a house
where feasting took place (the royal hall of Rohan)

Mering Stream. dial. "fixing a boundary" (stream forming an
eastern border of Rohan)

Meriadoc. Celt name *Mariadoc* (a hobbit)

Michel Delving. ME "great diggings" (a major town in the Shire)

Mithe. OE *mithe* "to escape notice" (the outflow of the Shire-
bourne into the Brandywine River)

Mordor. OE *morthor* "murder, torment, mortal sin"; Sindarin
"black country" (the Black Country of Sauron)

Mundburg, Mundberg. OE *mund-beorg*, an actual OE compound
word meaning "sheltering hill," appearing in the text in the
form Mundburg. The index to *The Lord of the Rings* gives
the form Mundberg, and the translation "guardian fortress";
probably both the fortress and the hill on which it stood were
referred to, and the references became separated (the name
in Rohan for Minas Tirith)

Náin. Icel. *Náinn* "corpse" (the name of three Dwarves, two of
them kings)

Nár. Icel. "corpse" (a Dwarf)

Nobottle. obs. *bottle* "dwelling, building" (a village in the Shire)

Numen. L "a divine or presiding power or spirit"; Quenya "west-direction" (the west, which, in the trilogy, was the abode of divine powers)

Oatbarton. "oat-farm" mod. *oat*, OE *bere-tún* "barley-enclosure." Tolkien has, consciously, followed the unconscious practice of combining incongruous elements in place names in applying an element referring to barley to the cultivation of oats (a village in the Shire)

Oin. Icel. Oinn "fearful" (the name of a king of the Dwarves and of one of Thorin's companions)

Oliphaunt. obs. "elephant"; mod. "an elephant-ivory trumpet." The word is retained in a surname (a mammoth type of elephant from Harad)

Olorin. OHG *Alarûn;* ON *Olrun* "a prophetic and diabolic spirit, a mandrake root" (Gandalf's name in the west in his youth)

Orald. OE "very old" *or* "original, early" (Bombadil's name among men)

Orc. OE "demon" from L Orcus, the Roman god of the dead (a member of the evil goblin tribes)

Ori. Icel. "raging one" (a Dwarf of Thorin's company)

Orthanc. OE *orthanc* "intelligence, skill, mechanical art"; Sindarin "mount fang" (Saruman's tower)

Púkel-men. OE *púcel, puckle* "a demon, goblin, or woodwose" related to the Irish *púca* "sprite" and to Shakespeare's Puck (sculptures at Dunharrow that resemble Woses)

Radagast. Slavonic *Radegast, Radihost* from *rad* "glad," *radost* "joy." The Slavonic god of bliss, good counsel, and honor, associated with the Roman god Mercury and the Greek god Hermes, traditional god of alchemists (a wizard)

Rethe. OE *réthe* "savage, cruel, fierce" (the hobbits' name for March)

Riddermark. OE *riddena mearc* "land of riders" (Rohan)

Rudigar Bolger. OE *rudu, gar* "ruddy spear" (a hobbit)

Rushock Bog. mod. "little-rush bog" *-ock* a diminutive from OE

-oc, -uc (a marsh in the Shire)

Samwise Gamgee. OE *sam, wís* "half wise" (a hobbit). The pun
between Gamgee and Cotton is that "Gamgee bandage,"
named for the surgeon who developed it, is gauze over cotton
wool

Saruman. OE "crafty man" *searu* "craft, device, wile"; the word
can be used in a good or a bad sense (a wizard)

Scary. dial. *scar* "rocky cliff" (a village in the Shire)

Scatha. OE "malefactor"; compare *scathe* (a dragon)

Shelob. "She-spider" ME *she*, OE *lob; lob* and *cob* are both from
OE *coppe* "spider" originally meaning "pendulous." *Atter-
cob* means "poison spider," compare *adder* (a giant she-
spider)

Simbelmyne. OE *simble, myne* "evermind" (white flowers that
grew in Rohan where the dead were buried)

Smaug. Norwegian, form of *smyge* "slip, sneak, steal" (a dragon)

Sméagol. OE *smeah* "penetrating, creeping" (Gollum)

Smial. OE *smygel* "a burrow, a place to creep into" (a hobbit-
hole)

Solmath. OE *solmonath* "February"; *sol* may mean "mire" (the
hobbits' word for February)

Southlinch. mod. *south*, ME *linch* "to burn or give light" (a type
of pipeweed)

Southron. Scot. "belonging to or dwelling in the south"; especially used of the English as distinguished from the Scots (a
man of the south, of Harad)

Staddle. dial. "the foundation of a building, barn, shed" (a village
in Bree-land)

Standelf. OE *stán, delf* "stone digging" (a village in Buckland)

Starkhorn. OE "stern horn"; *steark* "stern, unbending" (one of
the White Mountains)

Stoor. dial. *stour* "numerous, bulky, stout, sturdy, stubborn" from
OE *stor* (the tribe of hobbits that were the stoutest and
heaviest in build)

Stybba. OE *stybb* "stub, stump" (the pony that Meriadoc rode in Rohan)

Swertings. ME "swarthy ones" (the men of Harad)

Thain. mod. *thane*, OE *thegn* "a member of one of several ranks between earls and freemen" (a ruler of the Shire)

Thengel. OE *thengel* "a prince" (a king of Rohan)

Théoden. OE "chief of a nation or people" (a king of Rohan)

Théodred. OE "people's counsel" (son of King Théoden)

Théodwyn. OE "person, delight of the people"? (woman of Rohan)

Thorin Oakenshield. Icel. *Thorin* "bold one," *Eikinskjaldi* "with-oak-shield"; names of two different Dwarves in the *Prose Edda* (the Dwarf who led the expedition to recover Erebor from the dragon)

Thráin. Icel. *Thráinn* "obstinate" (the name of two kings of the Dwarves)

Thrihyrne. OE "three horn" (the mountain above Helm's Deep in Rohan)

Thrimidge, Thrimilch. OE *thri-milce* "May" (the hobbits' name for May)

Tindrock. OE "tine rock"; *tind* "tine, spike, tooth of a fork" (an island above Rauros)

Vala. Scand. "a seeress"; Sindarin plural *Valar* (divine guarding, guiding powers)

Variags. Slavonic *Varyags*, a name for Scandinavian warriors. (allies of Sauron from Khand in the east)

Vidugavia. Goth. *Vidugáuja* a smith-god of the type of Weland, from Goth. *vidus* "forest," thus a forest deity. Note that the spelling only varies in the interchangeable letters v-u, i-j (a king of Rhovannion which includes the forest of Mirkwood)

Walda. OE *weald* "powerful, mighty" (a king of Rohan)

Warg. Scand. *varg* "wolf" (evil wolves that hunted with Orcs)

Wedmath. OE *weth, monath; weth* "mild, gentle" (hobbits' name for August)

Westemnet. OE *west, emnett* "west plain" (the western part of Rohan)

Westfold. OE "west earth" (a part of Rohan)

Westron. OE *westren* "belonging to or dwelling in the west" (the Common Speech, spoken in the West)

Wetwang. mod. "wet country"; *wang* "field, country, place" (marshes at the confluence of the Entwash and the Anduin rivers)

Widfara. OE "wide farer" (a rider of Rohan)

Wight. OE *wiht* "a creature, a thing, a whit" (a spirit, specter)

Windfola. OE "wind foal" (the horse that Eowyn and Merry rode to Minas Tirith)

Winterfilth, Wintring. OE *Winter-fylleth* "October" (the names for October in the Shire and Bree respectively)

Withywindle. dial. *withywind* "bindweed"; like the bindweed, the Withywindle followed a winding course and ensnared travelers in the spells of its malevolent trees. *Windle* also means "basket," and baskets are often made of willow withies, so the Withywindle Valley could be considered a basketwork of intertwined willows (the river running out of the Old Forest, with many willows along its banks)

Wold. ME "open, hilly district" (an area of Rohan)

Woses. ME *woodwose, wodwos*, OE *wuduwasa* "a satyr-like woods-demon." Tolkien translates *wasa* as "forlorn, abandoned person" and suggests that *wuduwasa* first referred to actual people who had taken to the woods for survival (primitive, forest-dwelling people in the White Mountains)

Wulf. OE "wolf" (a man of Rohan who temporarily usurped the throne)

Yulemath. OE *geóla, monath* "December" (the name in Bree for December)

BIBLIOGRAPHY

Beowulf, translated by Burton Raffel. New York: New American Library, 1963.

Bosworth, Joseph and Toller, T. Northcote, *An Anglo-Saxon Dictionary*. London: Oxford University Press, 1898.

Davidson, H. R. Ellis, *Pagan Scandinavia*. New York: Frederick A. Praeger, 1967.

Davidson, H. R. Ellis, *Scandinavian Mythology*. New York: Paul Hamlyn, 1969.

Elder, Edda, The, translated by Paul B. Taylor and W. H. Auden, notes by Peter B. Salus (dedicated to J. R. R. Tolkien). New York: Random House, 1969.

Frazer, Sir James George, *The Golden Bough*, 1 vol. New York: Macmillan, 1963.

Graves, Robert, *The White Goddess*. New York: Noonday Press, 1966.

Grimm, Jakob, *Teutonic Mythology*, translated by James S. Stallybrass, 4 vols. New York: Dover Publications, 1966.

Grimm, Jacob and Grimm, Wilhelm, *The Grimms' German Folk Tales*, translated by Francis P. Magoun and Alexander H. Krappe. Carbondale: Southern Illinois University Press, 1960.

Gregory, Lady Augusta, *Cuchulain of Muirthemne*. New York: Oxford University Press, 1970.

Lobdell, Jared, ed., *A Tolkien Compass*. La Salle, Illinois: Open Court, 1975.

Loomis, Roger Sherman, *Celtic Myth and Arthurian Romance*. New York: Haskell House, 1967 (first published in 1927).

The Mabinogion, translated by Lady Charlotte Guest. New York: E. P. Dutton, 1902.

MacCana, Proinsias, *Celtic Mythology*. New York: Hamlyn Publishing Group, 1970.

Malory, Sir Thomas, *Le Morte Darthur*. 2 vols. Baltimore: Penguin Books, 1973.

New Larousse Encyclopedia of Mythology. Buffalo: Prometheus Press, 1972.

Plato, *The Works of Plato*, translated by B. Jowett, 4 vols. New York: Tudor Publishing, 1937.

Sturluson, Snorri, *The Prose Edda of Snorri Sturluson*, translated by Jean I. Young. Berkeley: University of California Press, 1964.

Raglan, Baron FitzRoy Richard Somerset, *The Hero*. New York: Vintage Books, 1955.

Tolkien, J. R. R., *The Hobbit*. Boston: Houghton Mifflin, 1966.

Tolkien, J. R. R., *The Fellowship of the Ring*. Boston: Houghton Mifflin, 1965.

Tolkien, J. R. R., *The Two Towers*. Boston: Houghton Mifflin, 1965.

Tolkien, J. R. R., *The Return of the King*. Boston: Houghton Mifflin, 1965.

Tolkien, J. R. R., *Tree and Leaf*. Boston: Houghton Mifflin, 1965.

Tolkien, J. R. R., *The Tolkien Reader*. New York: Ballantine Books, 1966.

Tolkien, J. R. R., *Smith of Wootton Major and Farmer Giles of Ham*. New York: Ballantine Books, 1969.

Tolkien, J. R. R. and Swann, Donald, *The Road Goes Ever On: A Song Cycle*. New York: Ballantine Books, 1967.

INDEX